STIM

What people are saying about Stim:

"Very often stories about someone with Asperger Syndrome are written by an NS (non spectrum) observer. No matter how warmly they intend, there is always the coolness of distance, of outsider viewpoint. Not so with *Stim*. Written by an Aspie, for Aspies, about Aspies, Kevin speaks our language and has the same trials, mishaps and dreams. He observes everything around him and discourses upon it with legendary AS wit, which seems to be the product of literal thinking, social confusion and an innocent, analytical mind. I loved it." – **Rudy Simone, author of *Aspergirls*, *Asperger's on the Job*, the "*22 Things*" Aspergers books, and *Orsath*.**

"*Stim* is AMAZING. Positively the best book I've read in the past year. As the mother of an ASD sufferer, I was crying by page four. Kevin Berry captures both the pain and the joy of this unfathomable and confusing condition, providing us with rare insight into the everyday struggles of an Aspie. Robert's story is frustrating, shaming, poignant, and ultimately triumphant. *Stim* should be on everyone's reading list." – **Lee Murray, author of *A Dash of Reality*, the award-winning *Battle of the Birds*, and *Misplaced*.**

This is a work of fiction. Names, characters, places and incidents are products of the author's imagination or are used fictitiously and are not to be construed as real. Any resemblance to actual events, locales, businesses, organisations, or persons (living or dead) is entirely coincidental. The exception to all this is that the September 2010 earthquake in Christchurch, New Zealand, did actually happen.

Copyright ©2013 by Kevin Berry
www.kevinberrybooks.com
Twitter: @kevinberryxxx

ISBN 978-1492877110
Waspie Publishing

Cover design by Rebecca Berto, Berto Designs, bertodesigns.com

All rights reserved. No part of this may be used or reproduced in any manner whatsoever without written permission, except for brief quotations used in reviews.

This book uses UK spelling and punctuation conventions.

STIM

An Aspie New Adult novel
set in an earthquake zone

Kevin Berry

ALSO BY THIS AUTHOR

Kaleidoscope

The sequel to Stim
Available late 2013

CHAPTER ONE

My 'therapist' suggested I should write a diary to try to understand these turbulent emotions. That is because it is difficult for me to know what are emotions and what are not. All I have are the thoughts in my head—sometimes calm, logical and ordered, sometimes a combination of things I do not quite recognise, yet they seem to draw me unrelentingly into the deep like some theoretical ravenous sea monster. I guess those are the emotions. Whatever they are, they are hard to qualify, tricky to understand, sometimes near impossible to control. It is like trying to put one of those giant jigsaws together, but I have never even seen the picture on the box, so I do not know where I am with it or what it is I am trying to make. I also suspect I am missing some of the important pieces.

By 'therapist', I do not mean a real professional therapist, of course. I cannot afford one of those on my meagre student allowance and haphazard income from part-time jobs. I mean Chloe. She is my friend and flatmate, and she is taking first-year Psychology at university (yet again), so she must know something. Also, her father pays for her to see a psychotherapist. I suppose I am receiving some help by proxy.

Just like me, Chloe is an Aspie. That is what we call ourselves, those of us who have Asperger's Syndrome, which is the most common form of Autism. In addition to this

Autistic Spectrum Disorder (or Difference, as she likes to call it), she also has an eclectic assortment of other diagnoses, but these are probably wrong. She has at various times been diagnosed with ADD (Attention Deficit Disorder), GAD (Generalised Anxiety Disorder) and SAD (Seasonal Affective Disorder), amongst others. She is numerically and lexically dyslexic, and she is hyperlexic, so when I want to say something, sometimes I have to interrupt her. She advised me to do that. She might be other -exics or -axics as well, but she has forgotten about them if she is.

Anyway, Chloe copes quite well with the NS (Non-Spectrum) world, or NT (Neuro-Typical) world, as most people call it. It must be due to all the psychotherapy she has had. Some Aspies genuinely struggle to cope with the various facets of everyday life, because the social etiquettes of life are developed and maintained by NS people, and therefore some of them seem strange, uncomfortable or disturbing. We are the square pegs that do not neatly fit into the round holes of life without taking a battering.

I feel lucky and privileged to have met Chloe, as she helps me understand how to navigate the murky seas of the NS world, avoid drowning in the ebb and flow of emotions, decode the hidden meanings of clichés and idioms, and recite the common dishonest responses that are expected when exchanging social niceties. She has already learned to solve these interpersonal puzzles, you see. I do not know if she is just an exceptionally kind person, or if she sees me as some kind of psychology project, and I do not know how I could know this without her actually telling me, and I do not know how to ask. Apparently, NS people know these kinds of things without even thinking about them. How they can do so without being told, I do not know. It is bewildering to me.

Sometimes I wonder why, when there are so many words to choose from to convey something clearly, people do not say what they mean, or mean what they say, but instead talk in some kind of code which I do not actually get, but NS people do. There are times when I think they are talking a totally different language, in which the meaning is often as twisted and mysterious as the roots of some ancient oak tree, buried and creeping in an unknown direction, and I cannot perceive it or dig it out.

I need my routines, of knowing something familiar will happen and when and how and with whom. I cannot visualise what something is like, or how it would feel, that has not happened to me yet. All I can do is remember all the things that have happened, and find the ones that are most like whatever is happening now, and assume history repeats. Apparently, it does not exactly, but it rhymes, and that is usually close enough.

All I know is how I experience the world, and that I do not comprehend much of it, and that not particularly well. I struggle to see why people do what they do, and say what they say. And that is sometimes painful, but mostly it is okay. The world does not understand me either, and that is fine. Chloe is there to help me find a safe passage through the treacherous waterways of life, to navigate the tempestuous sea of emotions of other people without being overwhelmed and sinking. At the moment, anyway. I trust her entirely.

Anyway, Chloe said I should write a diary or journal, because I can think so clearly in words, even if I cannot vocalise them especially well. And I can write them and never forget what I wrote or when I wrote it or where I wrote it. I think words are beautiful, especially the ones with neat little letters that do not extend up or down above the others, like 'universe' and 'unconsciousness', because they look so tidy on the line. But it is not possible to write a whole book like that, though I believe one person wrote a novel entirely without the letter 'e'. I would not do that as 'e' is one of the letters I like.

If I write enough, and for long enough, my diary might take on a life of its own and evolve into some kind of book, like Bridget Jones's diary, or even a series of books, like Samuel Pepys's diary (he wrote ten years of detailed volumes). Perhaps Samuel Pepys had an entertaining life and wrote it all down. Or maybe he just did not get out much, had a vivid imagination and was terribly verbose. I cannot know this for sure because I was not there at the time.

Some diaries get transformed from a book into a movie... Chloe tells me that the most popular movies contain four key features, which are violence, sex, swearing and explosions, and she says they are the most popular movies because that is what NS people enjoy watching the most. She has cautioned me not to rely on movies as representing a true and accurate depiction of normal human personal relationships.

Nevertheless, those four elements are what my book, or diary, should contain, and this, therefore, will be challenging. I know little of violence and nothing of sex (though it is my intention to make this a special project of mine; this year I will investigate sex and even try to take part). The swearing will probably occur sporadically as I write this book. I do not know whether there will be any explosions. Hopefully they will not be in the house. If I am lucky, the sex will happen somehow (though preferably not the violence at the same time), as I do need it as one of the four essential things for the film adaptation.

I am jumping ahead too much, because I imagine things that might happen (such as a movie based on my diary, which I have not yet written), and it is scary because I do not know if these things will happen or not, and that creates uncertainty, which creates stress, which leads me to imagine even more things. This is fretful. Yet whenever there is uncertainty, I feel compelled to evaluate all possible outcomes. But then I feel overwhelmed.

The other problem for me is that Chloe says I should write about what I know, and I do not know anything much. However, I do know about her, and about me, and so I will write about us.

This is how we met.

The university café was not busy early in the morning and early in the term (it was only February), which is how I like it. More accurately, there were seventeen other students there. All of them sat together in couples or in groups of three or four, and most were talking quietly. The ambient buzz of conversation was a level I could cope with, not so loud that it made my head ring, as would be the case if the café were fully occupied. In fact, the degree of murmuring acted as a comfortable white noise that was somehow soothing, like the lapping of waves against the shore or a hair-dryer on full power in a distant room.

I sat at a table in the corner sorting out my timetable for the rest of the day. Not just lectures, but a list I had made to organise my coffee breaks, toilet breaks, meals, quiet-time walks and an errand to the pharmacy to pick up my prescription. I plan everything in detail like this, so I always know when and where I should be. I do this because it is calming and grounding.

A coffee cup sat on the table in front of me, with some coffee remaining in it. I am never sure whether to say half-full or half-empty, because NS people claim these words indicate whether the speaker is an optimist or a pessimist, even though half-empty and half-full mean the same, so I always say it contains some coffee, which is rather vague.

Chloe approached my table with the sure, silent movement of a stalking cat, a cup of green tea in one hand and a black leather handbag in the other, and sat on the nearest chair to my left. It startled me that someone sat next to me when so many other tables were available, and I reclined in my seat, scrutinising her closely while she was distracted with organising herself and the items she carried. I already knew her by sight, but I did not know her name at that point in time.

She was slim and had cobalt blue hair that dropped forward, almost covering her left eye and concealing her left ear. Her eyebrows were dyed the same striking colour. She wore a black sleeveless top and tight blue jeans. Three silver earrings decorated her right ear, and I wondered if her hidden left ear had the same. She wore piercings in her lower lip and another through her right eyebrow. I imagined she would have a nightmare of a time trying to pass through metal detectors at airport security.

She turned her penetrating gaze on me, her unfathomable eyes as green as the Pacific ocean on a cloudy day. I immediately felt out of my depth and looked away uncomfortably.

"You're in my Econ 101 class, aren't you?" she said slowly. "I've seen you sitting in the fourth row in lectures. Is that your major?"

"Yes," I replied, glancing at her. I was not surprised that she recognised me, though my clothes and appearance, in stark contrast to her own, are uniformly plain and dull. I always sit in roughly the same place in the lecture hall, and so does she, usually two to four seats to my left.

"I see you've got an Autism wristband. I don't see many of those around. Why are you wearing it?" she asked. She took a sip from her green tea and sat back in her chair, looking at me. I looked away again.

"I have Asperger's Syndrome," I said. "I wear it for Aspie Pride and to raise awareness."

She smiled. "I thought so. About the AS. Me too. My name's Chloe. I'm doing Econ 101 as a filler. And Computer Science. Mainly I'm studying Psychology." She leaned forward. "You know, I can't find anything about ASD in the whole curriculum? Like, how crazy is that? What's your name?"

"Robert," I said. I was aware my coffee was cooling, but I felt somehow cornered by her gaze. A chilling panic rose within me as I struggled to recollect any similar events from which I could devise a plan for social intercourse with her, and realised that I did not have any experience whatsoever of talking to attractive girls who sat down next to me without warning. I do not think it has ever happened to me before.

We were silent for a while. I started rocking slowly in my seat, gazing outwards at the other people in the café, who were talking animatedly amongst themselves. I wondered how they could have so much to say and why they were sometimes so spirited when talking, and yet convey so little factual information to each other with perfect ease. In my current situation (I did not want to call it a predicament), I did not know what to do, what not to do, what to say, what not to say. I call this 'social fog'. It is the old London pea-soup kind of fog, thick and impenetrable, enveloping nearly everyone I come across. Someone must be clear and honest with me, like a foghorn blaring through the mist, to counteract the possibility of my misconstruing what they mean.

Chloe opened her bag and took out a blue pen, which she started spinning horizontally between the thumb and forefinger of her left hand. As it whirled around like a helicopter readying for take-off, I stopped rocking and turned to watch it. It was deft and captivating.

"This wretched assignment," she said, sipping more of her green tea and spinning the pen wildly at the same time. "Not the Economics one. The Computer Science one. About Easter. Writing a computer program to work out the date of Easter Sunday in two-thousand-and-fifty. Have you done it?" She paused a half-second for another swig of her green tea and then pressed on without waiting for my answer, which of course would have been that I had not done it because I am not taking Computer Science. "I've done it, but I don't know which is the right answer."

"You worked out more than one Easter Sunday for two-thousand-and-fifty?" I looked at her, and she looked away. Her pen spun furiously.

"Western Gregorian or Orthodox," she said. "April tenth or April seventeenth. It's not clear on the assignment."

"Uh… It is the first Sunday after the first full moon following the vernal equinox. And I am not studying Comp—"

"Yes, but allowing for different time zones and the sidereal calendar, the dates can be a week apart. We're in Christchurch, but theoretically it might be different for someone in San Francisco. Never mind. Have you done the first Economics assignment yet? I haven't started it. I haven't a bloody clue what they mean by 'inelasticity of demand'. Stupid jargon. Sorry for the verbal diarrhoea, I'm hyperlexic as well as Asperger's. If you don't interrupt, I might never stop talking."

At that point, she did actually stop talking of her own accord. Presumably to breathe. At last I felt I could contribute. A conversation is always more comfortable for me when discussing something I know than when discussing something about which I know nothing.

"Inelasticity of demand is when the demand for something is comparatively unaffected by changes in its price," I explained.

"Such as coffee?" said Chloe, smiling and pointing at the cup in front of me. Her ability to speak, point and still spin her pen in her other hand was quite impressive.

"No, because if coffee goes up in price, some people will drink tea instead. Petrol is more inelastic than that. A better example is a life-saving drug—people will buy that at any price."

"Hmmm, interesting. Well, thanks, but I have to go. I've got a lecture in six minutes. Do you want to meet up again? Here? How about ten past four this afternoon? Are you unoccupied then?"

I consulted the agenda on the notepad in front of me. "No, I will be taking a walk then. How about four-thirty-five?"

"That's good."

Chloe stuffed the pen back into her bag and rose swiftly from her seat, shouldering her bag in one fluid motion. She departed without saying goodbye, leaving the empty cup behind her, contrary to café regulations. What a rebel.

I stared after her. In the few minutes we had sat together, I had managed eighteen seconds of eye contact with this attractive girl. I congratulated myself on this accomplishment. I had done well. In our encounter at 4.35 p.m., I would aim for a full minute or two.

CHAPTER TWO

Books read lately:
Liar's Poker – Michael Lewis (note: this is not about dishonest card sharks playing Texas Hold 'Em; it is a shocking and humorous account of the culture of a Wall Street investment bank...)

I call them my little purple and green friends. One a day—so simple, yet they work to produce a complete personal transformation as if by magic. I would never have believed what a difference they make to me. It is no wonder people call these anti-depressants 'happy pills'. I keep them in the bathroom cupboard, between Chloe's various meds and mood stabilisers and Stef's contraceptive pills. I hope we do not mix these up. At least one of us could have a nasty surprise.

These little purple and green friends have not been part of my life for long. Only a few months, in fact, but I now know that I need them as much as I need food and water to sustain me. They allow me to be myself, whereas before my happy pills, I experienced a shadowy existence in the world, barely noticed, scarcely taking part and expending most of my energy on battling my own negative thoughts, an army of ghouls inside my head.

Every year it had become more and more difficult for me to fit in at school for no ascertainable reason. Sure, I was smart enough, but I found it difficult to make and keep friends because they generally considered me weird, clumsy and disinterested. It was not that I did not want to be friends, but that I did not know how to make it happen.

I gradually became more aware of the chasm between how I was and how others seemed to be. Ultimately, the day-to-day effort of trying to grow into the person I thought I should be (that is, more like the others) took its toll on me. I became quieter, withdrawn and alienated. I felt like I was always swimming against the tide, or walking into a raging gale. This, I suppose, was the start of the slippery slope descending into the abyss of depression.

One person helped me, which was a wonder to me, as I did not even realise that I needed help. I had just thought: this is the way I am. Different. Perhaps sad, if that is the right word. Alone. Feeling cold in a world in which so much warmth is shared amongst others. Plodding along in the dark when all around me is light, but my way alone is not illuminated.

Doctor Meg is a true friend. She saw what was happening to me, and she knew what to do. And this is how it happened, four months ago, at the end of my last year at school.

Meg is a young doctor in her first placement as a General Practitioner. She has long blonde hair, and a smile and a manner of talking that has always been able to put me at ease. It was Meg who referred me for my formal ASD diagnosis, and she supported me in understanding and coming to terms with it. She is by far the best doctor I have ever had. The others seemed interested in nothing more than prescribing me antibiotics occasionally and sending me on my way. But Meg cared like the truest of friends.

One afternoon, I was in her office grumbling about stress. The final school exams were coming up, and then I would go to university to study economics. I planned to leave the home I shared with my mother and move into the halls of residence at the start of the term. Both of these were significant life changes for me and, inevitably, the source of a lot of anxiety. Also, I was more aware than ever of the stark differences between me and others my age, and the thought of my recent Asperger's Syndrome diagnosis weighed heavily on my mind, like the burden of Atlas on his shoulders. Except perhaps at a time when Atlas had suffered a slipped disc or an acromioclavicular joint strain or something. I was apprehensive about survival in the new, free, adult world of university.

"Well, Robert," said Meg, tapping diligently into her computer before swivelling her chair, facing me and smiling broadly, "I think it's about time that we tackled this problem head-on. It's not uncommon for individuals with Asperger's. In fact, it's probably more common than not."

"What is?" I said, not even looking up. My attention was focused on an unidentifiable spot on the floor between my feet. It was not a particularly appealing spot, but I studied it intently nevertheless. It seemed harmless. I wondered if the stain was from blood or other body fluids.

"The 'D' word. Depression. Do you hear what I'm saying, Robert?"

"Yes," I murmured, hearing what she was saying, but not quite taking in the meaning of her words. It takes me time to process new concepts, like an oil tanker trying to change direction.

"It's clear to me, Robert, that you are suffering from depression. Yes, I know you're under stress at the moment, but I've watched you cope with stress before, and this is different. I've seen a slow decline in your mood, in your state of mind. We need to reverse that."

I looked up. "Are you sure? What could be causing the depression? Is it the stress?"

"Probably not." She paused, then continued matter-of-factly. "There are two kinds of depression, Robert. There's the kind caused by environmental effects—bereavement, divorce, redundancy and other major life changes. That can be a lot to deal with, but it's temporary. And then there's the other kind. That is what you are suffering from."

"The other kind?" I was still struggling to grasp this idea. The thought of depression had never occurred to me. I only knew about it from advertisements on the television, which proclaimed it was more prevalent than generally suspected, but could be helped.

"This sort of depression is caused by a chemical imbalance in the brain. It's not your fault, Robert. There's nothing you could have done to prevent it. Some people are just affected this way, that's all. It's an accident of nature."

"Are you saying that this is...a mental illness?"

"Yes, it is a mental illness, but it's fully treatable, and you don't need to see a psychiatrist. I can prescribe for you. In fact, most people respond very well to medication. We just have to find the right medication for you." Meg's smile never wavered. She could have been talking about her latest holiday in the Maldives rather than mental illness.

"But why do you say that I have this sort of depression?"

"You've told me that you feel listless, lack energy and motivation, and feel that you have nothing to look forward to in life. That every day is a battle with yourself, even to do ordinary things like shopping or studying. That you have trouble sleeping, and that minor things upset you out of all proportion to their importance. That you are living in the dark, that you feel isolated, anxious and worthless. That you do not understand the point of being alive. Well, the correct medication will make those feelings go away. I'm going to prescribe you a generic SSRI."

I had nothing to say to that. For all I knew, everyone had those same thoughts. This, in fact, was the first time that someone had suggested to me that thoughts like that were abnormal.

Meg retrieved a leaflet from her desk drawer and handed it to me. I took it and scanned it quickly. SSRI stood for Selective Serotonin Re-uptake Inhibitor. It was a class of drug that slowed the removal of serotonin from the brain.

"Serotonin is one of the neurotransmitters in the brain acting to control mood and common functions like eating, sleeping and thinking," said Meg as I read the leaflet. "It's a natural chemical which your body produces itself. However, in some people it gets absorbed too quickly."

"Why did you not prescribe this before?"

"We can't, Robert. It's not indicated for persons under eighteen. Now, though, before you start university, I think you should try it. A word of warning, though—you might feel worse than you presently do for a couple of weeks, but afterwards things will improve, so stick with it. If we start the medication now, by the time you begin university, you should feel a lot better."

"Sure," I said, perking up a little. My head spun like a mini tornado on ice with the news that Doctor Meg thought I was mentally ill. On top of my ASD diagnosis, this was a lot to accept, but the medication sounded quite promising. "Are there any side effects?"

"Sometimes there are, especially at the beginning, in the first couple of weeks...minor things like diarrhoea, nausea, headache or anxiety."

"Really? They sound very unpleasant."

"They usually go away quickly." She leaned forward on her desk and lowered her voice, though why she did so I do not know, as there was no one else in the room to overhear. "Some people experience some sexual dysfunction. Let me know if anything like that happens. We can change your medication."

"I cannot do that," I said.

"It's completely confidential."

"But I have not ever had sex."

Meg leaned back in her chair and smiled again. "Ah, well, there is no hurry for that. There is plenty of time for that. A young, handsome man like you won't have any problems in that department, I'm sure."

"I am going to make it a special, personal project of mine next year, after I start university," I said.

"A project? I'm not sure I understand you... Oh, do you mean, you hope to find a partner?"

"A girlfriend, yes," I confirmed. "That is my special project. Find a normal, attractive girl to go out with. Not a girl with AS. I want some part of my life to be normal."

"I see."

"I have written it down on my plan for next year already. There is time for a girlfriend in addition to my economics study."

"I don't think it is something you can plan out just like that, Robert. These things happen when you aren't expecting them, generally."

"That sounds inconvenient," I said.

"Why don't you just see how it goes?"

"All right," I said, a bit unsure of myself, as usual, and not truly understanding Meg about this. *See how what goes?*

"Come and see me again in three weeks, and we'll evaluate how you're getting on with the medication. We can always adjust the dose if necessary. The normal dose is one to three pills a day, but if you need more than one, it doesn't mean that you're more depressed. How much you need just depends on how your body assimilates it. And if you take more than you actually need, the body just absorbs it, so it's not a problem."

"That sounds fine, then," I said. "I will do it."

And that is how it started. One little purple and green pill a day, every day. The first two weeks were miserable, as Meg said they would be, but after that, I felt much, much better. My irritability was gone. I no longer had a sense of hopelessness about the future. I stopped wishing that I was dead. My anxiety about leaving home and starting university subsided. I started to enjoy some of the little moments in life, like walking under the trees, reading, and looking at the beauty in nature, instead of feeling stressed all the time and vocalising how I was a failure who did not deserve to live. I even started smiling. I felt so different, and everyone around me treated me differently, more nicely, as a result.

That is why I call them my little purple and green friends. But the reality is that they enabled me to begin to make friends myself.

Chapter Three

Books read lately:
Devil Take The Hindmost – Edward Chancellor (note: this is not a religious text in which the Prince of Darkness captures straggling sinners; it is a history of stock market speculation over the past 300 years...)
Number of sexual encounters:
None

Meeting Chloe in the café became comfortingly familiar and as regular as clockwork. On Mondays, Tuesdays (twice), Thursdays and Fridays, we convened in the café—nearly always at the same corner table, whenever we could occupy it, and with the same drinks—like déjà vu stuck in some kind of unstoppable time loop. On a few occasions, the time passed without either of us saying anything, but somehow comforted by the other's presence. Sometimes we talked about our studies or assignments, but mostly we talked about ourselves. Or more accurately, I should say Chloe talked about herself. She had been entirely truthful about the verbal diarrhoea. Words spilled out of her mouth with a rapid staccato, machine-gun-like rhythm.

But I did not mind this. When I was in the café by myself, I could only observe people interacting socially, try to work out what was going on in their minds and what it was they were doing, to try to unravel the mystery of their behaviour. I never actually knew what was going on with them, could never properly interpret what I observed, because I could only imagine. Invariably, people behaved inconsistently and did not do what I expected or wanted them to do, and I could not discern any patterns underlying their actions. This was confusing, sometimes bewildering.

With Chloe, it was all very easy. She just poured herself out to me, wholly and honestly and clearly, and I lapped it all up like a thirsty kitten drinking cream from the saucer of knowledge. For the first time, I had a friend I could understand, and who could understand me, because we seemed to communicate on the same wavelength. I think she felt the same, but she never said exactly.

Chloe told me all about herself, how she had been first diagnosed when young, and passed from doctor to doctor and psychiatrist to psychiatrist, collecting the acronyms of different diagnoses like alphabet soup until finally she was evaluated with Autism Spectrum Disorder (ASD). Once she knew that, she sped-read numerous books on the subject, assimilating their collective wisdom. The very best, she told me, were those written by fellow Aspies who had struggled to fit into the NS world but ultimately prevailed to establish their own place within it somehow, and yet remain true to themselves. Chloe said she could identify with their early lives, and that everything in her own life, past and present, made sense to her after reading those books. She had always known she was different, and now she understood why. And I agreed with her. I borrowed the books and read them too. I felt the same.

Chloe explained that her father travelled a lot on business and tried to make up for his frequent absences by ensuring that she always had the best care possible. Evaluations. Psych tests. Personality tests. Private mental hospital whenever she felt especially distressed. A seemingly interminable tweaking of her medications (eleven different *combinations so far) in an attempt to find the right mix and dosage, a kind of educated guessing on the part of her doctors. There is so little known about the human mind in general and the Aspie mind in particular. It is so complex that all the doctors can do is just try one thing at a time, pick up the pieces if it does not work out as planned, and try something else, trying to solve the incomplete jigsaw of a fractured human mind.*

One day when she met me in the café, my life changed forever.

Her leather bag suddenly clonked onto the table, and a moment later Chloe slid smoothly into the chair next to mine. She was wearing tight jeans and a black sleeveless top again, because this was a Tuesday. She always wore that on Tuesdays.

I laid down *How I Made $2,000,000 in the Stock Market* and looked up at her. By now I was much better adjusted to her presence, and generally comfortable maintaining eye contact with her.

"I've had enough of the halls of residence," she declared vehemently. "Noise, noise, noise, parties, more noise. It's too distracting. I can't sleep, study or work on my website. It's such a pain, and I'm getting out. My cousin Stef rents a house in Matipo Street, and her two flatmates have just left. She has to replace them quickly because she can't afford the rent for the whole house on her own. I've decided that I'm going to take one of the rooms. There's one other. It's fully furnished—desk, bookcase, chest of drawers, firm bed, one window—east-facing—soft carpet, not at all scratchy, beige walls without decoration. Are you interested, Robert?"

"I am," I said automatically, then considered for a moment. I had also become irritated with the level of noise and constant activity in the halls of residence. There were simply too many people in a small space, all coming and going at unpredictable times. Change is hard for me, but sometimes it is necessary, and I recognised that this was one of those times. At least I knew Chloe well enough now, and my schedule at university would remain the same, so I considered it likely that I could cope with the change of abode. "The beige walls sound good," I continued. "Nice and bland, not at all over-stimulating."

"Great. Stef's fine, she's cool. I'm ninety-nine percent sure you'll like her. She's not AS, but she's very understanding. I've already told her about you, Robert. She says it'll be great, for once, to have two quiet people in the house. Her last flatmates were dire. Bogans, she said. They got behind on the rent because they spent all their money on drink, music and mobile phones. The landlord forced them to leave eventually, and Stef has promised to choose her new flatmates more carefully. She asked her sister, but Marinda didn't want to move from where she is, and she's going to buy a house soon anyway."

"But why does she want us?" I quipped.

Chloe glared at me, stunned, for a couple of seconds before she burst out laughing. "I think she wants two people who are absolute polar opposites of the last two. That's why we're in."

"Thank you for asking me, Chloe. I think you will be a super person to flat with. I like being with you. You are quiet, clever and fun too."

Chloe smiled. "You too."

So that was settled. Apparently, we could move in later that week, and we discussed the cost. I could afford it, barely. I have a part-time job as a shop assistant to earn a little money each week. It is dull, but it does pay the bills. At least, it sometimes pays some of them.

"Let's get some drinks and muffins to celebrate," said Chloe, springing to her feet and lifting her bag at the same time. I left my book on the table to retain our place, so we could return to the same seats. I did not think anyone would take it, as few students have money to invest on the stock market (including me—my interest was purely academic), so the book would be of no use to them. We made our selections—a cappuccino (three dollars fifty) and an apple and cinnamon muffin (four dollars twenty) for me, and a blueberry muffin (four dollars) and green tea (three dollars seventy) for Chloe.

I did not recognise the woman at the till that day, which was a little disconcerting, because I always like to see the same people in the same place doing the same jobs. But that was just the beginning of our trouble."

"Eleven dollars forty, please," she said to me.

"No," I replied.

"That comes to eleven dollars forty," she repeated, as if I had not spoken at all.

"The total cost is fifteen dollars forty. You have not charged us for the blueberry muffin."

She checked the docket. "Hey, you're right. Thanks for pointing that out. A lot of people wouldn't have said anything. That'll be fifteen dollars forty then, please."

"We are paying separately. Mine is seven dollars seventy."

She rang it up wordlessly. I gave her a ten dollar note. I always pay in cash, because I like the look of coloured banknotes and the feel of hard coins in my hand. It is somehow more real to me than credit.

She gave me twelve dollars thirty cents in change.

"You have given me change for twenty dollars," I said, holding the change out in front of me. "I gave you only a ten dollar note. Are you having a bad day? Are you sick or something?" Though I felt irritated by her inaccuracy, I thought that maybe she was ill or stressed or something was affecting her concentration. "Do you need a doctor?"

She snatched back the two five dollar notes she had given me, leaving me with the correct change. "Of course I don't need a doctor. I'm not ill. Maybe they should give you my bloody job," she grumbled. I saw her nicotine-stained teeth and smelled peppermint on her breath. Perhaps it was a dentist she needed.

"No." Why she suggested that I take her job, I did not know. I thought it best to refuse. "You should stop smoking. Your teeth look horrible."

"Yeah, well, who bloody well asked you?" she said, slamming the cash register drawer closed. "Have a nice day."

She asked Chloe for the correct amount, also seven dollars seventy cents. Chloe, as usual, paid with her credit card. As she has dyscalculia, a kind of numerical dyslexia, she never trusts herself with cash. She sometimes transposes the numbers and often cannot ascertain if she receives the correct change if she pays with cash. And she always signs for things because she either cannot remember her PIN or enters it in a jumbled-up order. Telephone numbers are as alien to her as the moons of Jupiter (of which I think there are sixty-four known). I had to enter my number into her phone for her when we exchanged contact details.

We sat in our favourite spot to plan our move into the house to share with Stef in Matipo Street. However, I was already becoming anxious about it in some undefinable way. It was like a slow-forming dread, an uneasy feeling that fed on uncertainty. Though that was nothing compared to how I would have felt prior to starting the anti-depressants, when the mere consideration of a lifestyle change of this scale without considerable advance warning would probably have induced another panic attack.

We thought it would be easier if we each helped the other to shift our belongings, and we decided to move into the house on the Friday afternoon, which, unfortunately, turned out to be a stiflingly hot day with a gusting north-westerly wind. We had no car, and did not like the idea of making two trips by bus from Ilam to Riccarton with boxes of stuff, as that would be quite cumbersome, and it is actually an easy walking distance. It would not seem right to take the bus such a short way. The best solution we could devise for this problem was to go to the Pak 'N' Save supermarket in the Mall at Riccarton and borrow two shopping trolleys for a few hours.

We pushed these back to the halls of residence, which was a distance of 2.5km, taking the path along University Drive through the university itself. There appeared to be a concert on outside the Student Union building. The music was quite overwhelming, and it drowned out whatever the students shouted at us from across the river. Why they were shouting, I did not know, and Chloe said she did not care.

First, we packed Chloe's stuff into the trolleys—two boxes of clothes, a box of books and her laptop—and pushed them back the way we had come through the suffocating heat, past the Mall and down to our new home in Matipo Street. It was hot and arduous work, and we proceeded without talking, as there seemed to be nothing to say at this point, as we both knew what we were doing.

Besides, we were breathless.

Stef was at work (she works as an accounts clerk in town somewhere), but she had left us house keys under the doormat. We took the boxes inside and put them into the room that Stef, with a post-it note stuck to the door, had denoted was for Chloe.

The temperature seemed even hotter than before as we pushed the trolleys back the same way to collect my belongings. My feet dragged as if I were wading through golden syrup with a ball and chain attached to each of my legs. I tried to imagine that we were trudging through some endless desert somewhere, but it obviously was not a desert, it was a main road lined with P30 parking signs, and the shopping trolleys were probably marginally easier to push along the footpath than through the sand. They did seem to have a life of their own, though.

The concert outside the Student Union still proceeded noisily and apparently quite chaotically, and if we were heckled again, I did not notice. This was because I felt too exhausted to look. My shirt and Chloe's top were wet with sweat and sticking to our skin.

We loaded my things into the trolleys—one box of clothes, my laptop and two boxes of books. I collect books like a dragon reputedly hoards riches. They are my little treasures, though I cannot afford to buy them often, and I usually acquire them second-hand. I love it that a book can be relied upon to provide the identical information, or tell the same tale, time after time—unlike people, who can be fickle. Rereading something I already know is grounding for me, and it is pleasing to know that information in a book is always the same each time I look at it.

It was now late afternoon. The trolleys were not easy to handle, not having been designed for long-distance pavement journeys, and squeaked continuously, making me grind my teeth in annoyance. Chloe stimmed by tapping out a beat on the handle of her trolley as we walked, the regularity of which was reasonably calming. Sometimes, one of the trolley wheels would stick and drag along the footpath with a high-pitched shrieking until it freed itself. Other times a wheel would turn randomly, causing one of the trolleys to lurch sideways abruptly, like a pouncing metallic cat. However, we managed the almost 3km back to our new home without serious incident.

After the constant noise and bustle of the halls of residence, it seemed positively tranquil in the new house. I got my first look at my new room. It was a comfortable size, 4.7m by 3.9m, and well laid out, almost a clone of Chloe's room in size and shape. Chloe had the room next to mine, then there was Stef's room, and one bathroom, which we would all have to share. Chloe announced that she would draw up a colour-coded timetable for the bathroom for the three of us each morning and evening. I appreciated that careful planning on her behalf. That was one more detail arranged (and one fewer thing about which to be anxious).

We unloaded my possessions and took them into the house. Chloe bent over and carefully placed a box of books on top of the one that I had put down next to the bookcase. As she stood up, she wiped the perspiration from her forehead with her left hand. She wore a white sleeveless top (because this was a Friday), and sweat gleamed on her arms and shoulders. Her blue hair was tousled, and I wondered if she felt as worn out by the heat as I did. One strap of her top had fallen down her right shoulder, but she ignored it, or perhaps was unaware of it. She took three steps to my bed and lay down, letting out a heavy sigh. She twirled her hair with her left hand, and patted the bed with her right hand.

"Robert, why don't you sit down here? You must be tired. You could rest a while too, lie down, maybe. We could talk or...you know, something."

I thought I knew how she felt, though, of course, I could not know for sure without Chloe telling me. This was a significant move for us both, bringing a lot of change and, inescapably, anxiety. As she rested, I looked eagerly at the empty bookcase, already mentally arranging my books in order by category and (within that) alphabetically by author. I felt a surge of excitement as I anticipated removing them from the cardboard prisons of their boxes, feeling the smooth dust covers in my hands, and placing their regular rectangular shapes neatly onto the white shelves in front of me in a perfectly ordered, systematic manner.

Chloe sighed again. Perhaps it was because she realised she would have to unpack also, and felt too tired to do so. Suddenly, I realised that we had missed our break together at the university café because we had been too busy moving into the house. I felt thirsty. A cold drink would be good, but a hot drink ought to be better. Apparently, hot drinks cool your body down faster than cold ones.

"Do you want to go out for a coffee?" I asked her.

"I don't drink coffee," she said abruptly, then sat up, stood and left the room. A few seconds later, I heard the door of her room close.

That is right, I admonished myself. Chloe drinks green tea. No wonder she did not want to go out for a coffee.

Chapter Four

Books read lately:
When Genius Failed – Roger Lowenstein (note: this is not about clever students who unexpectedly flunked exams; it is the story of a hedge fund run by Big Names, including two Nobel prizewinners in Economics, which spectacularly lost $4.6 billion within four months in 1998 and put the entire financial system at risk...)
Number of sexual encounters:
Zero

There is a well-known equation, known as the Drake Equation, that is used to estimate the number of detectable, sentient, communicative races in the galaxy (besides us, if we consider ourselves as one of them). It works (or does not work, according to its critics) by guessing the value of a lot of variables, such as the fraction of stars which have planets, and the fraction of planets which develop intelligent life, amongst other things, and multiplying them all together. Depending on the values chosen, the equation produces a number between zero (we are alone in our galaxy) to billions (we have lots of intelligent neighbours in the galaxy).

I decided to modify this equation to estimate the number of potential girlfriends for me in Christchurch. Here is my Girlfriend Equation, for a Scientifically Calculated Reckoning of Eligible Women (or SCREW score):

$$G = P \cdot f_w \cdot f_a \cdot f_i \cdot f_s \cdot f_p \cdot f_r \cdot f_h \cdot f_g$$

where

 G = the number of potential girlfriends for me in Christchurch;

 P = the population of Christchurch, which is about 400,000 (I am not interested in a long-distance relationship, so I am restricting this variable to my home city);

 fw = the fraction of the population made up of women, which is about 50% (I am not interested in a gay relationship, so I will calculate for females only);

 fa = the fraction of the above women within one year either side of my own age, so aged about 18-20, which I estimate at about 5% (I do not want to date a schoolgirl, and women aged 21 or over will surely be too sophisticated for me);

 fi = the fraction of the above women who are highly intelligent, say with an IQ within the top 5%, which is (obviously) a certain 5% (because we must be able to talk to each other at approximately the same level);

 fs = the fraction of the above women who are currently single, which I...um...guess is about 50% (I do not want to date someone already dating someone else, as I do not want to get involved in threesomes or a trinogamous relationship);

 fp = the fraction of the above women who I find physically attractive, which is...er...about 10%, at a guess. I do not know exactly (I think physical attractiveness is probably quite important for the sex aspect of the relationship);

 fr = the fraction of the above women who reciprocally find me physically attractive, which is even more difficult to estimate...so about 20%, at a guess (yes, this is double the percentage I estimated I find attractive, but I am not unhandsome, you know);

 fh = the fraction of the above women who I will like

hanging out with, which I estimate at 100% (I am sure I would like hanging out with an attractive woman, and I am quite easy-going);

fg = the fraction of the above women who will get along with me and tolerate my Aspie ways... Hmm, hard to estimate... I will be generous and guess 20% (most women are likely to consider me too weird to go out with, as Chloe told me).

Treating all of the above as independent variables, which is maybe a little questionable as some of them are probably correlated, I plugged all of the values into the equation, which became:

G = 400000 x 0.5 x 0.05 x 0.05 x 0.5 x 0.1 x 0.2 x 1.0 x 0.2

Multiplying everything together, this equation of somewhat dubious credibility results in:

$$G = 1$$

That is it. I have calculated there is one unattached, intelligent woman of about my age in Christchurch who I will find physically attractive and who will find me physically attractive, and enjoy hanging out with. One.

Where is she?

It was Saturday morning before I encountered Stef for the first time.

I was standing outside the bathroom door, memorising the colourful and detailed timetable Chloe had pinned to it, when the door opened abruptly and a young woman barrelled out through it, busily texting on her Android phone and not looking where she was going. I tried to move out of her path, but clumsily I stepped the wrong way, and we collided. She sprawled face-down on the ground, sending her phone cartwheeling three times across the carpet before it came to rest.

"I thought you were stepping left, I mean, to my right,

your left," I explained, while she scrambled on the floor to retrieve her phone. "But actually you were going the other way, and that is why we collided. I was reading the sign on the door, and I did not know you were about to come out of there."

She got to her feet. "That's okay. You don't need to explain. Anyway, I wasn't watching where I was going. In a rush, busy busy as usual!" She smiled broadly and extended a hand towards me. "You must be Rob. Welcome to the house. I'm Stef. Pleased to meet you at last, Rob."

"My name is Robert," I said. I smiled back, but under the force of her unfamiliar gaze, I refocussed my eyes on the spot on the carpet where her phone had briefly lain. I realised that I was supposed to grasp her hand with mine and move it rhythmically up and down. I do not like touching people whom I do not know, but Chloe has told me that this is a social ritual I need to become adjusted to performing, so I reached out my hand and let Stef touch it, though it felt clammy, and I said 'Hi'.

She stepped back, increasing the distance between us, and said quietly, "Have you settled in all right?"

"Yes, thanks," I replied and looked directly at her. She was attractive, a little older than Chloe and I, with shoulder-length curly mahogany hair. Chloe, in her role as my unofficial therapist, had trained me to maintain eye contact whenever possible, as NS people prefer eye contact for thirty to sixty percent of the time when they are talking with someone. I was getting better at this now, following the series of desensitising exercises she had led me through, starting with imagining making eye contact with a friend, to actually briefly doing so, then with strangers, then increasing the frequency and duration of eye contact until I could manage social norms in most circumstances. It nearly always works, but is less effective with complete strangers, and does not work at all with aggressive or intimidating people. I cannot look at them without experiencing sensory overload.

"Hey, I've got time for a coffee or something before I rush off, if you want to talk, ask me anything about the house or whatever, or just chill out. If you want to, that is."

"Okay," I said warily. I could not think of anything I immediately needed to know about the house, and I was not feeling too warm, so I did not need to cool down either. However, it would be useful to practise my conversation skills. Chloe had told me to practise these whenever possible, even when I had nothing to say, to help me fit in to the NS world. It is called 'tiny talk' or something.

We went downstairs to the kitchen, where we each made a coffee. Chloe had explained to me earlier that all the food in the house was for sharing unless it was labelled otherwise, as this was the easiest option. Stef explained she did not mind what system we wanted to use. I felt overwhelmed by these alternatives and said whatever was simplest would be acceptable to me, and Chloe's one seemed reasonable. We took our drinks to the kitchen table, a rather dilapidated piece of furniture with disconcertingly mismatched chairs, and sat down.

"Chloe said you are studying Economics. How are you finding that?"

"Oh, it is at the university."

"No, I meant, is it interesting?"

"Yes, it is an interesting subject, but the course so far is very basic. I have read all of the textbooks already, so I have started reading about economics in history. I do not know if there is a name for studying that. Maybe econohistory or historonomics... Anyway, it is fascinating."

"Uh-huh." Stef leaned back in her chair, which creaked

in protest, and took a sip of her coffee.

I continued, as the history of economics was a subject that I found engrossing. "I have just finished reading *Extraordinary Popular Delusions and the Madness of Crowds*. The first two chapters are about two of the greatest asset bubbles in history, Tulipmania and the South Sea Bubble. You see, people started trading options on tulip bulbs on ten to twenty percent margin in sixteen-thirty-six in Holland. As tulip trading became more fashionable, the price continued to rise, and more and more people were drawn into the tulip market, until everyone wanted to trade on tulips. Extraordinary deals were made, with people exchanging vast fortunes for a few tulips. For example, at the peak of the market, a brewer exchanged his entire brewery for just three tulip bulbs. Shortly afterwards, the whole market crashed, many people were bankrupted, and the country entered a depression."

Stef's eyes had glazed over a little, I assume with the intense concentration she had on what I was saying. She continued drinking her coffee, and she glanced at her watch. When she looked back at me, her expression had changed slightly, but I did not know what that meant, so I continued. I felt so excited to have someone to talk to about economics and economic history. I thought I might call it 'historonomics' after all.

"And then the South Sea Bubble—that is really interesting, particularly pertaining to the situation today. In about seventeen-twenty, The South Seas Company purchased the UK government's debt, converting it into shares, some of which were given to politicians, who then were incentivised to drive the share price higher with rumours of extravagant profits to be made. Investment frenzy took over as the share price went sky-high, and the company even lent money to investors to buy the shares, driving it higher still. Other nefarious companies were listed for eager investors to buy into amidst this frenzy, and then the whole fraud collapsed, and lots of people lost a lot of money. It was even proposed in parliament that bankers be tied up in sacks filled with snakes and thrown into the Thames, an old Roman punishment. Some of the—"

"Sorry for interrupting you, Robert, but I've got to go. I'm meeting Jeff for lunch. I need to leave now." Stef drained the rest of her coffee quickly.

This disrupted my train of thought, and it took me several moments to take in what she was saying, during which time I sat there with my mouth open, completely still.

"Jeff?" I eventually managed.

"My new boyfriend. I'm meeting him for lunch, and I need to get ready. You know, put on my make-up to look attractive for him, and so on."

"Oh, you do not need make-up to look attractive, Stef—you are pretty just as you are."

She smiled at me, her teeth gleaming and her earrings flashing from the sunlight streaming through the kitchen window. "Thank you, Robert, that's very kind of you to say."

"It is not kind, it is true. Anyway, I can tell you more about the South Sea Bubble when you get home. And the Mississippi Scheme. I am so glad you are interested."

"Um... I'm planning to wash my hair when I get home. Well, gotta go. See you later." She left the table and went back upstairs. I continued to sit there, finishing my coffee and thinking about the South Sea Bubble. A short time later, Stef came downstairs with a small green handbag, rushed past me, said 'Cheerio—have a nice day' and went out the door, slamming it closed behind her.

I glanced at my watch, which was a more elementary

model than Stef's Swiss one. 10.34 a.m. Perhaps she planned to have an early lunch today. Or maybe she had to drive all the way to Akaroa to meet her boyfriend.

Stef and Jeff, I thought. That has a neat sound. Curious how one is spelled with a single 'f', and the other is spelt with a double 'f'. I smiled. It always felt good to notice things like that.

I stayed at home most of the day, spending my time reading *The Zurich Axioms*, completing an assignment, rearranging my books on my bookcase again—I was still trying to find the most pleasing arrangement—and talking to Chloe.

This was the first full day in our new home. Chloe told me that she felt quite stressed. She always wears a red beret when she is stressed, as she experiences the tightness of it around her head calming somehow. She said it helped when I told her that I had also felt stressed, but relieved this by zoning out with two hours alone reading and shuffling my books on the bookcase. New home, new surroundings, new routines—I need quiet time to adjust, to take it all in, to acknowledge and accept the changes. So does Chloe. But I do not know why she felt better when I said I had been stressed too.

We sat on old orange fabric sofas in the living room, discussing our move to the flat, our studies, our interests, and how crazy the NS world sometimes is. Chloe had her feet on the coffee table (does she think of it as a green tea table?) and whirled a pen in her left hand. I lay on the other sofa, twitching my right foot against a cushion every few seconds. I like to do that. The gentle tap of foot on fabric is predictable and self-soothing.

Like this, relaxed, we had a really enjoyable talk, Aspie to Aspie. It is somehow much more comfortable for me than talking to NS people, probably because I find Chloe's style of communication clearer and more straightforward.

Time passed quickly. After a while, we started discussing our flatmate, Chloe's cousin Stef. I did not know her, so Chloe did most of the talking. As usual.

"Stef's all right, you know. And her sister Marinda too. We all went to the same school, but Stef was four years ahead. She looked after me. When I used to stim or squeal in class and all, the teacher would send for Stef to try to explain what I was doing that for. You know, long before I knew I was Aspie and suspected bipolar and diagnosed ADD and other alphabet disorders, before I understood myself and learned ways to look after myself. Stef already realised I needed my own space, you see, control over my environment and all that. I wasn't like the other girls at school. All they did was hang around in groups and talk about boys and TV shows and clothes and stuff. Do their hair. You know. And all that 'hi, what cool shoes, you look great, have a nice day' crap. And they touched each other all the time! It made me want to puke. And they thought I was a geek! Just 'cause I used computers a lot and played the violin! But Stef understood me. She gave them hell if anyone gave me problems."

I nodded. At this point in the conversation, I had pretty much lost all faith that I would get to say anything before Chloe started off again, hence the nodding. But this time she surprised me by pausing for a few seconds, so I jumped right in.

"Stef has gone out with her new boyfriend, Jeff," I volunteered. "We were having a great talk about historonomics, which is a term I have just invented, and then she said she had to go out."

"She changes boyfriends more often than I reinstall

Windows on my laptop. She's always on the phone to one of them. I can't even remember their names. And she must have, like, two hundred friends on facebook. Who needs that many friends? But she's all right, really." In the background, I heard the front door opening and closing. "She's a bit disorganised and chaotic. And she isn't the least bit obsessive."

I nodded again, absent-mindedly thinking of disorganisation and chaos, and how I like to convert it to order. Chloe fiddled with her dangling blue hair, rolling it between her fingers. Some NS people simply flit from one thing to another, like drifters lost in a haze of social trivia. I was grounded in my economics. Chloe in her music and her computers. We knew where we were with these things, and more importantly, *who* we were. Though, from time to time, our fixations would change.

At that moment, Stef walked in carrying shopping bags containing two shoe boxes. "Hi, guys, who's not obsessive? Were you talking about me? I'm obsessive about everything! Especially shoes! Do you want to see my new red Italian low-heels?"

"No," said Chloe.

"How is it possible to be obsessive about everything?" I asked, puzzled. Surely there is only enough room in your head to be obsessive about one or two things at a time. Unless maybe NS people have more space. Or have a lower obsession threshold.

Stef laughed but did not answer me. She pulled out the shoe boxes and showed us the red shoes anyway, and another pair that were black. She had just bought them both. That puzzled me too. Why would she want to get more than one pair of shoes at a time?

"Hey, guys, I'm going to my friend Marianne's for a

party tonight," she said, putting the new shoes back in their boxes. "Are you interested in coming? No pressure or anything. I know it's probably not your thing, but you're welcome to come if you want. Marianne asked me to invite you and everything."

"No," said Chloe immediately. "I don't like lots of people. Or the noise. I'll stay home and work on my web app."

"Web app? I did not know you were designing a web app," I said. "What is it for?"

"It's an idea I'm trying out. I'll send you a link. You can test it for me if you like. That'd be cool."

"Robert?" prompted Stef, standing by the doorway with her bags of shoe boxes. "How about you?"

"I am not designing a web app," I said.

"No, I meant Marianne's party. Do you want to come? I mean, I guess not, but—"

"What happens at Marianne's parties?" I asked abruptly. In the old days, when I was depressed, I could not even imagine going to a party. I would have had a panic attack. Now, with the happy pills that Doctor Meg had prescribed, I wondered if I could handle it.

"Oh, you know, meeting people and stuff. Listening to music. Drinking. Chatting. I met my last four boyfriends at Marianne's parties."

And, therefore, it may be where guys meet potential girlfriends, I thought.

"I'll introduce you to some cool people I know. There's a quiet girl called Teena who'll be there. You'll probably like her."

"That might be nice. I want to have a girlfriend, a normal girl, not with AS or ADHD or STD or anything. Finding a girlfriend is my personal project for the year."

Stef regarded me with a strange and undecipherable expression for a few moments. "Well, I'm sure you two will hit it off."

This confused me. "Is she violent?"

Stef laughed. "No, Robert. It's just a figure of speech. It means I think you'll like each other."

Chloe stopped whirling her pen. She slammed it down onto the coffee table, then got up and left the room. I think she probably wanted to get back to designing her web app.

"Great," I said to Stef. "I will come with you to Marianne's party."

CHAPTER FIVE

Books read lately:
Barbarians At The Gate – Bryan Burrough and John Helyar (note: this is not about the Sack of Rome in 410 by the Visigoths, led by Alaric; it is an expose of greed, manipulation and reckless conduct in 1980s New York investment banking...)
Number of sexual encounters:
Nil (but becoming hopeful)

I have been wondering:
   Why is there no ham in a hamburger?
   Why do our noses run and our feet smell?
   Why is it that people suffering from stress are said to be cracking up, yet are breaking down?
   Why, as French Fries came from France, did English muffins come from America and Danish pastries come from Austria?
   Why is it when 'oversee' means to watch and monitor closely, 'overlook' means the opposite?
   Why is there only one Monopolies Commission?
   Why is it when your odds of success are slim, you have a fat chance?
   Why is it that horrible things are horrific, but terrible things are not terrific?
   If someone says 'a penny for your thoughts' and you 'put your two cents in', what happened to the other cent?

We went in Stef's little green car, a Mazda that was probably older than her. I call it 'The Frog', because (1) it is green; and (2) it sometimes makes a noise like a frog, and hops like one, when Stef changes gears.

Marianne lives in Linwood, which is just on the other side of town. We left home at 8.17 p.m., but by this time I had become quite anxious about being at the party, and I started rocking back and forth in the car to try to use up some of that nervous energy. Stef noticed this and stopped The Frog on Gloucester Street.

"Robert? Are you okay? If you've changed your mind, I can take you back home, if that's what you want. It's cool either way."

I glanced outside. It was dark, the stars were obscured by clouds, and it probably was chilly outside. I closed my eyes and rocked steadily, thinking about how far I had come since I had emerged from the oppressive fog of depression and learned how to overcome some of the non-social traits that my ASD had imbued me with. Here I was, in a car with a woman I had met only that day, on my way to a party where I would know no one else, with the aim of meeting someone to become my girlfriend. Though how that would work, I had no idea. I could really only plan one step at a time, and it was too difficult for me to imagine the consequences of any of the steps. Going to the party would be challenging enough, like a prisoner walking into the Coliseum arena to face the lions.

"Robert?" prompted Stef, who had been waiting patiently. The car was still running, and the left indicator was ticking nicely and regularly. It was quite transfixing actually, and I had synchronised my rocking with it.

The lure of the possibility of finding a girlfriend was strong enough for me to overcome my fear of the situation.

I desisted from rocking. I took a deep breath, looked directly at Stef and said, "It is very thoughtful of you to ask me how I feel and if I am okay with this. I will go with you."

She smiled and nodded in return. "I'll introduce you to Teena when we get there. She's quiet too. Maybe you can ask her about her work. And she likes walking and reading books. You can talk to her about walking and books."

"Those are good ideas, thank you. I have been reading a lot about economics lately. I can talk about that, too."

"Hmm, perhaps not so much," replied Stef.

She reversed the indicators, glanced in the mirror, stomped mercilessly on the accelerator pedal, and we set off again. About five minutes later, we arrived. There were a lot of cars outside Marianne's house, which was easy to identify because seventeen young people were standing outside drinking from bottles and music was blaring out of the living room windows. Stef managed to squeeze The Frog into a small parking space farther down the road with considerable skill and a little swearing.

Apprehensively, I followed her to the house. My palms were sweaty, and my breathing had become strong and deep from nervous tension. We went inside. There were eight people in the hall. Stef greeted some of them briefly as she went past, but I did not say a word. I lowered my eyes and forged a way through after Stef, who seemed to get past the bunches of people congregating in the hall much more easily than I did. I bumped into some of them. Already, my senses felt overloaded due to the noise and the number of people. Inside, the music coming out of the living room was deafening, with a beat that made my head pound and my ears hurt. I imagined that I could feel the noise vibrating the muscles in my stomach, making me feel a little nauseated.

Thankfully, we did not enter the living room, which was heaving with people dancing jerkily in unpredictable ways in response to the music. I did not know if I could have gone in there. I could taste bile in my throat. Stef went past into another room, the kitchen. I followed like I was tethered to her with an invisible lifeline.

Stef turned to face me. "I can't see Teena in the living room or kitchen. If you wait here, I'll check the study. Maybe you could get us some drinks, Robert?"

Before I could respond in any way, she slipped past me back into the hall. I felt abandoned and distinctly uncomfortable in this bizarre environment. As I looked round, I could see the other people in the kitchen paid no attention to me, and I relaxed slightly, then tensed up again as I realised I could not see any drinks in here. Two people were standing in front of the refrigerator, so I would not be able to open it.

I remembered seeing a table laden with drinks and snacks in the living room as we passed the door. I returned there uneasily, chewing my lip. There they were, on the other side of the room, perhaps five metres away, a trivial physical distance but a monumental mental one. I shuddered and bravely took my first step into the room. Music blared at me so loudly that I could actually feel it pressing against my skin. People writhed, jived, jiggled and giggled around me. My head felt like it was spinning to the dizzying beat of my heart.

I bumped heavily into a young woman in a green top twirling around a man with spectacles wearing a 'Crusaders' rugby shirt. She stumbled, and the man caught hold of her arm to steady her.

"Watch where you're going, bud," he said to someone, looking at me. I didn't know who Bud was. I hoped Bud would not bump into me, because I had been having enough trouble as it was.

I continued to the drinks table, threading my way between another dancing couple, and fortunately reached it without further incident.

There were a lot of bottles of beer and a bottle-opener but no glasses. *How can people drink without glasses?* I thought, and I looked around, but no one seemed to have a glass. Some people held the bottles between their fingers. Perhaps they were waiting for glasses.

I decided to return to the kitchen to look for glasses, but as I turned around, I bumped into the woman in the green top again. She had moved from where she had been dancing, and I had not been able to hear her coming because of the raucous music.

"What's your problem, mate?" said Rugby Shirt, stepping in front of me.

"Glasses," I said, looking away from him for a way past. He was blocking my path.

The man touched his spectacles with a podgy finger. "Had too much to drink already, have you, mate?"

I did not answer. He could not be talking to me. I was not his mate, and I had not had anything to drink. I looked for a way around him, but I couldn't concentrate. The noise and the blurry movement of people dancing in the dimmed light of the living room were too much for me. I felt anxiety rising within me to the point of panic. I was ready to bolt but could not see a way out, like a horse who discovers the stables is on fire when the door is closed. A familiar voice in my head suddenly urged, *Get out of here, Robert.*

Rugby Shirt reached out and pushed my right shoulder roughly. "Want a piece of me, bud?"

"Leave him alone, Bruce", said the green-top woman.

I saw a gap appear and moved jerkily into it, bumping into another man. I felt utterly overwhelmed now. Focusing my vision narrowly ahead of me, I moved forward, brushing past other people, reached the hall and then the front door. Cool air breezed against my face and through my hair. I rushed through the front gate, almost at a run, the feeling of panic subsiding with every quick step away from the mass of people and the blasting music. As I walked rapidly down the street, I felt control returning to me. I realised I was breathing hard, and it was not from the walking.

I had tried to do too much. The situation had been well beyond anything I could handle yet, even on my anti-depressants. Of course, I had thought that I might be extremely uncomfortable in that environment. People with Asperger's usually are. That was why Chloe had stayed home. I had simply hoped that the anti-depressants would make it easier to cope. But they had not.

I walked on, deciding to go home on foot to allow my head to clear. It was still throbbing painfully.

I remembered Doctor Meg saying the anti-depressants would free me. She had said that the normal dose was one to three pills a day, and that if I take more than I actually need, the body just absorbs it. I decided right then and there to increase the dose to see if it would help me more. I currently had seventy-two pills remaining of my current prescription. I would start taking two pills every morning, and go and see Doctor Meg earlier than usual for a new prescription, as I would run out of them in half the time.

It would take me an hour and a half to walk home, but I did not care. The cool air and the light drizzle that had just started were refreshing. I was alone now, and that was exactly what I needed.

CHAPTER SIX

Books/articles read lately:
Macroeconomic Policy and the Optimal Destruction of Vampires – Dennis J Snower (note: this University of Chicago journal article covers what it says it does...with mathematical models too...)
Number of sexual encounters:
None yet :-(

I have also been wondering:
Why is it that people say fish 'n' chips, but never say chips 'n' fish?

Why is it that people say knife 'n' fork, but never say fork 'n' knife (does that sound rude)?

Why do they say 'n' instead of 'and' anyway?

Which came first—the chicken or the egg? Surely it must always be the chicken. Chickens can run, but eggs cannot move.

Why is it that people who are not much to speak of are the most fascinating to talk about?

Do clocks go 'tick tock' or do they actually go 'tock tick'?

How come night falls but does not break, yet day breaks even though it never fell?

How come there are never any stories about the three little wolves and the big bad pig?

I started the day after the party with my first double dose of my little purple and green friends, followed by a quick breakfast of coffee and toast with Marmite, for I had to rush out to my Sunday job, which was at a department store in town. It was not much of a job, or much of a department store for that matter (in fact, it is actually not much of a town anymore). I did not see either Chloe or Stef before I left home.

I took the bus. Through experimentation, I have developed a system of sitting, or rather slouching, on the seat in the bus and glaring at the floor of the aisle, so that people rarely, if ever, sit next to me. I do not like people sitting next to me on the bus, for I like to sit by the window, and if someone sits next to me, I start to feel claustrophobic and cannot easily get out. Also, I do not like them touching me, and if a fat person sits next to me, they inevitably touch me. So I deliberately sit in a way that usually makes people look for another vacant seat.

I reached work on time and was assigned to the women's department that day, for they had two staff off sick. I was given the undemanding task of minding the changing rooms, which involved counting how many garments a customer takes into the changing rooms, giving them an appropriately numbered tag and then verifying that the tag and number of garments match when they come out. I actually did not need to use the tags because I could easily remember how many garments each customer had taken in, but I had been instructed to follow the process, so I did.

My work there was devoid of drama (and completely without interest of any kind) until 12.17 p.m., when one of the customers, a plump middle-aged woman, came out of the changing rooms wearing the blouse and trousers she had taken in to try on. She went over to a man sitting down on a couch outside the changing rooms put there for the purpose of allowing men to rest. I had noticed him watch women go in and out of the changing rooms. He seemed to be an extremely observant person.

"What do you think, Rodney? Do you like the blue? Or would black be better? They say black never goes out of fashion. And the trousers? Do they look too tight?"

"Blue's fine, dear, and the trousers too," said the man, who was possibly her husband. I noticed how quickly he was able to assess the suitability of his wife's choice of clothes, for he simply glanced at her for a moment before swivelling his gaze back to a tall blonde woman trying on an impractical pair of shoes.

"Pay attention, Rodney. This is important. I simply can't wear clothes that make me look dowdy. Now, are these trousers fine, or should I try on the striped ones? Stripes are slimming, you know. Or maybe you don't know. But of course if I go for the striped trousers, I can't have the blue blouse. I would have to have the black one. Or a white one. Are you listening, dear?"

Another brief glance back. "Yes, dear. They're fine. Don't fret."

"I'm not fretting. I'm very particular about my appearance. It must be just right." She turned to present a profile view to her husband, who was not watching anyway, and hissed, "Does my bum look big in this?"

"You look fine, dear," said the man, concentrating intently on a young woman browsing through the cardigans.

"Oh, you're hopeless," said the woman. She spun around to face me. "You look like a sensible young man. What do you think of this outfit?"

I considered for a moment, intent on being as helpful as possible.

"Your bum does look big in those trousers," I said. "It quite bulges out, in fact. I think you should choose a much larger pair. The blouse also. It looks very tight under your breasts."

I arrived home at 1.07 p.m., having been fired from my Sunday job in the department store for gross misconduct and told never to return, even as a customer. I genuinely did not know what I had done wrong. I had been helpful and honest. The manager explained to me that there is a time to be honest, and there is a time to sell clothes, and I did not know the difference. I honestly did not understand what he meant.

Music wafted from the living room. Elgar, I think. Chloe was sitting in there playing her violin. She stopped playing and asked me why I had come home early. I did not feel like telling her, but I did anyway. I focussed my attention on the floor as I recounted the events, so I would not get distracted and miss out some detail.

"What jerks," she said, fiddling with the bow of her violin.

"Who? The manager or the customers?" I asked, looking up at her.

"All of them. I mean, they ask you a question, and they don't want to hear the answer if it disagrees with their own opinion. Typical NS crap. I've heard this heaps of times."

"But not everyone is like that," I protested, hoping that I was right; otherwise I may as well take a vow of silence and join a monastery. "Anyway, I thought I was being helpful. It would have been rude not to answer, and wrong to lie."

"I know what I'll do," said Chloe, turning to face me directly with her piercing green eyes. "I'll write a description of this and post it onto *hate list* for you. In the 'just today' section."

"*Hate list*?"

"My web app. I sent you a link as I said I would. Haven't you checked it out yet, Robert? I emailed you the link early this morning."

"Sorry, no, not yet."

"Well, it's *hatelist.net*. I've sent you a username and password and instructions and everything. I've linked your account to mine too. I'm still developing the web app, so it doesn't have all the features yet. It's cool, though. You get a 'permanent' *hate list* and a 'just today' *hate list*. The 'just today' list is for you to nominate anyone who's really pissed you off today. If you don't know their names, you can write a description or upload a photo. The 'permanent' list is for those people you perpetually hate. It's really cool."

"It sounds interesting. Can you show me later? Now, I really just want to get a coffee."

I went into the kitchen to make one. Ninety seconds later, when I was pouring the milk, Chloe joined me in the room.

"How was the party?" she asked.

"Horrible. I lasted only four minutes." I grimaced and took my coffee back into the living room. Chloe followed me like a shadow. She perched on the side of the sofa while I sat down on the front edge and leaned forward. It was one of those sofas like a big rectangular marshmallow that you feel you could disappear into, never to re-emerge, if you lean back too far. Perching on the front edge was probably the least uncomfortable position.

"Stef said you must have left the party quickly because she couldn't find you. You just took off, didn't you? Was that before or after meeting her friend Teena?"

"Before," I admitted sadly.

"I don't try to go to those things anymore. They make me feel like a mouse out of its cage, surrounded by crazed cats conducting a cacophonous yowling concerto. And then I always feel so bad afterwards for having gone there in the first place, and worse for skulking away the first chance I could. That overwhelming sense of discomfort becomes an overpowering sense of inadequacy and disappointment, and I just feel like shit."

"That is pretty much how I felt. And miserable. That is why I am increasing my anti-depressants dose, up to two pills from today."

"Be careful," warned Chloe.

"Doctor Meg said it would be all right. I just wanted to try to fit in at the party. You know, pretend to be normal."

"Why the fuck do you want to be normal, Robert?" said Chloe, springing to her feet. She started pacing up and down in front of the sofa. "No, no, no. Well, okay, sometimes you have to put on the happy face and spout the appropriate social responses at the correct time, but you also have to let the real you come out the rest of the time, or else you've lost yourself. You've got to know where your strengths and weaknesses are. I've told you that, remember? Before going to the party, you felt sick, right? Nauseated? Trembling? Racing heart? Sweaty? Not hungry?"

"Yes, I did," I admitted.

"Recognise your triggers. Listen to the warnings. Start with something easier than one of Marianne's parties."

"Sure," I agreed weakly. This felt like a lecture, but I knew that Chloe was right. The truth was that I would have found pulling out my own toenails preferable to staying at that party even half an hour.

"Look," said Chloe, her voice quieter now, and she sat down next to me, perched on the front edge of the sofa, hands clasped in her lap. "Before I started therapy, I couldn't even sit in a café if someone was sitting at an adjacent table. Now I'm fine with that. Take little steps."

"I can do the mirror now." Since starting my little purple and green friends, I had been able to look in a mirror for the first time, though still only fleetingly. Before that, I would sooner have stared at Medusa on a bad hair day.

"That's what I mean. Baby steps." She paused. "You only went to the party because you wanted to meet that girl Teena, didn't you?"

"Yes. That is why I went. Stef thought we might like each other. I really want to have a girlfriend, a normal girl, you know what I mean. I planned for it this year, and I thought I have to try—"

"That won't be easy," said Chloe, which I did not find reassuring in even the least respect. "NS guys don't mind weirdo Aspie girlfriends because it's cool to have a quirky girlfriend. But NS girls don't like weirdo boyfriends. And I don't mean that we're weirdos, just that that's what NS people think we are. I don't think you're going to find an NS girl to be your girlfriend, Robert. She'd have to be really desperate."

"Thanks, Chloe. That really makes me feel better." This seemed like the appropriate point in the conversation to use sarcasm.

"You're welcome," she said obliviously. "She'd think you're an odd one. Your future girlfriend, I mean. If you have one, and if she's NS. It might take her a while to get used to your Aspie ways."

"I know. That's why I've bought a copy of *22 Things A Woman Must Know If She Loves A Man With Asperger's Syndrome*. It's like a user manual that I can give to her."

"Sure, but why do you want a girlfriend anyway?"

"I do not know what sex is like, and, well, it might be good."

Chloe stared hard at me for a few seconds. I do not know why. It was very unusual for her to take so long to think of something to say.

"I don't know what it's like either."

"But you said that NS guys like quirky girlfriends."

"But I don't like them!"

I considered this for a few moments while Chloe twiddled her dangling hair and stared across the room at some unidentifiable point.

"So...you have not had sex any time either?" I ventured.

"No. All I really know about it is what I've seen on television and in the movies. I don't understand it. There doesn't seem to be any pattern to it. I don't get it."

I sighed. "I do not get it either."

We heard the front door close and, four seconds later, Stef came into the living room, dropped her handbag on the floor by the other sofa and threw herself onto it lengthwise, where she lay on her back, her head resting on a blue cushion.

"Whew! I'm exhausted," she said, wiping her hand across her forehead. "I had lunch with Marinda, then we went window shopping. I was good and didn't buy anything. I'm worn out now, though!"

Why would Stef be shopping for windows? I wondered. We did not require replacement windows. No windows in the house were broken.

Lying on her side, Stef turned her head to look at Chloe and me as we sat perched on the front of the other uncomfortable sofa together. "You guys look cosy. What are you talking about?"

"Sex," said Chloe.

Stef's face reddened. I understood why she said she was exhausted. Obviously, she had been in a hurry, and that was why her face was flushed.

"Um... Maybe I'll just go—"

"But you just got home," I said, "and you look tired."

"Yes, you should rest a bit," said Chloe. "You can tell us about sex. We don't really know anything much about it. Only what is in movies and books and on TV and such. And that's not very conclusive. I mean, how do you know that you're not doing it wrong?"

"Er..."

"What is it like?" I asked. "Is it like the movies?"

"Um... I dunno. Maybe. Depends what movies you watch, I suppose."

"It is not like *Fatal Attraction*, is it?" I asked. I was pretty sure it was not like that, but thought it best to clarify. "You know, where after sex the crazy woman comes and kills your pets."

"How about in *Amelie*?" asked Chloe. "That didn't look like much fun."

"Well... It's kind of different," said Stef, looking redder than before, which I thought was strange because she was now resting. "Didn't your parents tell you about this stuff when you were younger?"

"Hell, no," said Chloe. "They told me something about the physiology of it, of course. I don't know much about what it's supposed to feel like, but at least I think I know where the personal bits are meant to go."

"I did not even get told that," I complained. "I had a four-minute sex education lecture from my mother, but the word 'vagina' was not in it. I had no idea where the man's penis was meant to go for two years after that. I kind of worked it out by watching *Bridget Jones's Diary* on TV."

"Shit, Robert, that's bad."

"I liked that movie, actually."

"No, no," said Chloe. "I meant it was really bad you didn't get told much about sex. I mean, how else are we supposed to know? I suppose you didn't get told about orgasms either?"

I shook my head.

"Me neither. It was ages until I learnt that was the nice bit that sometimes happens at the end. But is it actually nice? I mean, what you see in movies and on TV doesn't always look that nice. Stef, what's it like?"

Stef was lying on the other sofa, staring at us with her mouth wide open like she was about to scream, but she did not do that. For a few seconds, she said nothing, then said, "Um... Who would like a game of *Monopoly*?"

Stef and I quickly talked Chloe into it. I can never resist a game of *Monopoly* because I really like handling the money. Not because it represents money. I like the mental arithmetic that goes with it, and it was a unanimous decision that I should be the banker because of that. We played the *Here and Now* edition, which is fantastic because the numbers are large. Chloe complained that she would not be able to handle the numbers, so I said I would help her with that. Stef looked after the unsold properties. She said she has always wanted to trade real estate, but this was the closest she had got to it.

We played for ninety-seven minutes before Stef said she had to go and get ready for going out with Jeff later. We left Stef's position as it was (in case she came back later) and carried on with the game, just Chloe and I. We played longer and longer, taking only brief stops for toilet breaks. My head was spinning so much with the constant mental arithmetic that from time to time I passed in and out of a trance-like state, a period of distorted time and intense focus. We appeared evenly matched as we gradually built up our property empires. And the bank kept dispensing £2m every time we passed 'Go'. I reasoned that this was inflationary, and so it proved.

After a while, we started trading properties between ourselves. I sold Gatwick Airport to Chloe for £14m, which was seven times its nominal value. In return, I bought British Telecom from her for £10m. At that point, we decided (or rather, I decided, and Chloe just went along with it) that the rents were too low now in relation to our exalted moneyed status, so we quadrupled them.

A little while later, the Bank of Monopoly ran out of money, but rather than stop playing, we considered our options.

I was in favour of allowing a recession to occur and tightening fiscal policy, perhaps by paying a proportion of rents to the bank, and abandoning the £2m 'Go' payouts for a while, thus allowing the *Monopoly* economy a natural period of readjustment, during which the Bank of Monopoly could recapitalise itself.

Chloe, however, was in favour of just printing more money. We could do that quite easily by creating new banknotes with coloured paper. We (or rather, I, because of

Chloe's dyscalculia) would write the new figures on these, and we would simply give them to the bank. Instinctively, it felt wrong to me to conjure up new money simply by printing it, but Chloe explained that if it was okay for the Bank of England and the U.S. Federal Reserve to do this, then surely we could follow their example and implement our own form of quantitative easing.

So we did that. I created the extra money with some coloured paper and a ballpoint pen while Chloe went off to the kitchen to make us a couple of sandwiches, because it was dinner time. I heard Chloe swearing because the condiments were not lined up in the correct sequence in the pantry, and it occurred to me that it was less trouble for me to make a few billion dollars out of coloured paper than for her to put the sandwiches together. We ate them while we played, finding room for the bread plates and glasses of water amongst our highly-ordered piles of properties and *Monopoly* money. Stef came home, saw we were still busy with the game, and went upstairs without a word.

We played on into the evening. Now that we knew we could simply create money as needed, there was no impediment to our continued enjoyment of the game. Our strategies were different. I would hoard banknotes, whereas Chloe would spend regularly on property expansion. We soon realised there were not enough houses or hotels in our game anymore, so we went to the kitchen and got a bag of salted peanuts (houses) and a bag of cashew nuts (hotels) to continue building on our properties and escalate rents even further. The only downside to this was that occasionally we would eat a house or hotel (though we were only allowed to eat our own), but I guess that served to cool down the property market a bit.

When one of us was presented with a particularly hefty rent bill (and they were becoming quite large, as we had quadrupled them again), if we could not raise the cash, then we would merely exchange debt (an I.O.U., essentially) with the promise of paying interest on it every time we pass 'Go'. We called these financial instruments collateralised debt obligations (CDOs) for fun, but really they were not collateralised at all because they were each a single debt, so they were more like mortgages backed by... Well, we did not know. Nothing, probably. But we felt rich all the same.

We carried on playing late into the night, not so much because we were actually enjoying it, but because we no longer knew how to stop. We had the answer to any monetary problem—just create more credit. Or debt. They are the same thing anyway. But, finally, it was too much. At 11.24 p.m., I landed on Canary Wharf on which Chloe had constructed a veritable hotel empire of three ordinary hotels and seven cashew nuts. The astronomical rent was not beyond calculation, but it was beyond imagination. We decided to give up at that point and total our positions.

That took quite some time owing to the complexity of the financial arrangements we had made. It seemed that we had been exchanging debt backed by other debt. It was all tremendously complicated. However, by 12.53 a.m. we had a final tally. Chloe owed me £23 billion, but I owed her £175 billion. After determining this, we decided to declare Stef the winner, as her position, which had lain untouched for over nine hours, had cash and no debt.

It took a while to tidy the game away, even though we ate most of the houses and hotels. We considered saving our CDOs and IOUs for scrap paper but tossed them away because they seemed worthless. Whoever would need a note bearing a trillion dollars anyway?

At 1.17 a.m., I went upstairs, knocked on Stef's door (loudly, so as to wake her if she was sleeping) and went in. Chloe stayed downstairs munching on the last of the hotels.

"Stef, are you awake?" I turned on the light, so I could see whether she was awake or not.

"Mmphf?" A curled-up figure under the duvet groaned and slowly sat up. The duvet fell down, revealing Stef's tousled brown hair.

"We have finished the game. You won," I announced.

"What? Do you know what time it is?"

I glanced at her bedside clock. "That says one-twenty-one a.m., but it is a couple of minutes fast."

"You woke me up at this bloody time in the middle of the night to tell me that I won the bloody game?"

"Well, yes... I thought you would be pleased. Your defensive, traditional strategy really worked."

"I'm not pleased, Robert. I was asleep! Couldn't you have waited until the morning?"

"Um... I suppose so," I conceded.

She groaned and threw herself back in the bed, pulling the duvet up around her head. "Turn out the light on your way out."

CHAPTER SEVEN

Books read lately:
Whatever happened to Penny Candy? – Richard J Maybury (note: this is not a murder mystery novel in which a sweet young girl disappears; it is a fun and clearly-written book for children, introducing the principles of economics...). I also started four other books in the past two days, but could not get into them and put them aside.
Number of sexual encounters:
Still nothing

I had a few close friends when I was a school kid, though never more than one or two at a time, but my best and constant friend was Sam. He was always there for me, whether I needed someone to talk to, someone to give me advice, or someone just to keep me company quietly, and he never asked for much in return. Sometimes I would talk with him every day for days at a time, when he almost seemed to live in my house with me; at other times, weeks would go by before he talked to me again, but that was okay. It was always just fine. But I only hear from him occasionally nowadays.

Sam was intelligent, like me. He liked reading the same kind of books as me, too. We would read an entire series of three, four or five books consecutively, and we would discuss them for hours. If I discovered a new author I liked, we would read everything we could find by that author before picking up another book. We read through nearly everything we picked up, except the dictionary (I gave up on it because it kept changing the subject) and the telephone book (too many characters to follow). My other friends were okay to hang out with for a while, but eventually we would become restless or bored with each other's company, and part. Sam was there for the long haul.

It did not matter to him if I decided to spend my Saturday afternoon scattering my old 2000 AD comics all over the floor of my bedroom, then rearranging them in issue number order, or create an index of which issues and pages my favourite characters appeared in. It did not bother him when I spent months reading dry textbooks, trying to learn how to read cuneiform and hieroglyphics, or work out the family tree of the ancient Greek gods. Nor did he flinch when I spent three months memorising vacuum cleaner model numbers, past and present, to work out if that was interesting to do, or not (my conclusion was inconclusive).

I could always rely on Sam to help me, to give me sound advice when I was unsure what I was supposed to say or do in the NS world, to encourage me when I needed a little push to do something that I simply could not face doing by myself, like go somewhere I had never been before, or enter a crowded shopping mall, or speak to a new teacher. But sometimes Sam and I spent so much time together that it drove my mother to tears or to anger. She never understood Sam or how close we were, or why I needed him with me sometimes but not others, but she never heard any of the things he said that helped me so much to cope with family life, school and everything else. She never spoke to him at all, or saw him. That is what infuriated her about Sam, I think. That Sam was my best friend, and he was not real. He was my imaginary friend.

I knew he was pretend, of course. It did not matter at

all that he was a figment of my imagination. Sam was a voice in my head that I eventually worked out was a part of me, but it was a part of me that was not part of my outer personality, if you see what I mean. I do not think Sam has Asperger's Syndrome or any other neurological disorder. I think he is an amalgamation of what I have subconsciously assimilated from NS people of how they speak and act and react. I think he will always be there for me, when I need him.

I think it is okay to have an imaginary friend sometimes. Lots of people have them, but they might not admit it. I have often wondered if, when people pray, they are talking to their imaginary friend, God.

It was over two weeks since I'd doubled my dose of the anti-depressants, and I felt good. Truly fantastic. Better than I've ever felt before, actually, and I'd been feeling that way for two days now. I kept thinking, is this what ordinary people feel like all the time? If it is, then wow, it's incredible. And I had so much energy, I didn't need to sleep much at all. Just five hours a night seemed to be enough. I would go to bed late, at 1 a.m. or 2 a.m. after playing online computer games or reordering my book collection again, then get up early and go out for a run before breakfast.

Today, I'd already completed my run and was now at a loose end. I spent some time pacing up and down in the living room, my mind racing with all the possibilities of what I could do that day. I was alone in the house, as it was the university holidays, and Chloe had flown south to visit friends in Dunedin for a week or so. Stef was at work at the moment, and she had been spending some nights over at her boyfriend's house, so I had not seen much of her. It was odd having the whole house to myself, but I liked it. I could eat when I wanted (though my appetite had disappeared), sleep when I wanted (which was not a lot now) and watch whatever I wanted on TV (though everything on TV lately seemed to be rubbish, and I'd only been able to watch for a few minutes at a time before getting restless and switching it off).

On the spur of the moment, I decided to check up on Chloe's web app again. I'd finally got around to checking out *hatelist.net* a few days ago, and I thought it was pretty cool. I made a coffee, my second of the morning, set up my laptop on a small table in the garden, and logged on.

As usual, the title of the website had changed. I wasn't sure if this was due to Chloe's dyslexia or whether it was a quirky feature she had programmed in, but the title always seemed to be a different anagram of '*hate list*'. Last time it had been 'the tails'. Now it was 'a thistle'.

Typing fast, I added several former British Prime Ministers and ex-US Presidents to my permanent *hate list*. This, of course, was just out of basic principles. I certainly didn't know any of them. In fact, several of them had died before I was born. But I thought they deserved to be hated all the same. They must have done something wrong. People usually don't ascend to positions of power like that by being nice.

For a laugh, I added Stef's boyfriend Jeff to my 'today' *hate list*. I didn't really know why I did that. Maybe it was out of envy, because I knew he and Stef had been having sex, and I hadn't. Anyway, his name would be gone from the 'today' *hate list* tomorrow, so it didn't actually matter much.

Then I noticed that Chloe had introduced a new feature, the ability to add a generic group to the list. Quickly taking advantage of this, I added 'lawyers' to my permanent *hate list*. Again, I didn't have anything much to do with lawyers, but it seems that no one likes them, so I put them on the list. I thought a little more and added 'psychiatrists' and 'ministers of religion' too. I saw that Chloe had added 'doctors' to her list, but I like Doctor Meg, so I didn't do the same.

A brilliant idea suddenly occurred to me, and I jumped up from my seat. I could design my own web app. Chloe could program it, and we would make millions. With excitement, I paced up and down the garden, heedless of the foliage (which was mostly weeds, anyway), gesturing frenetically to the garden furniture as a flood of ideas swamped me.

There was too much to remember, and I ran into the house, searching for paper. The first paper I came across was Chloe's music score sheets, and I returned to the garden table with them and a pen. Some of the ideas were blatant rubbish, but a few were not bad. I liked IOUaPint.com, in which people could repay favours or make gifts to others of virtual pints (or glasses of wine, or whatever), and the recipient could redeem them at a local pub or restaurant, with the giver being charged for the drink by credit card. That would enable the internationalisation of the 'I owe you a pint' culture and actually allow people to receive the drinks they are given. Not a bad idea. I enthusiastically started drawing up web page layouts.

After a little while, I tired of that and browsed to an FX trading site that I'd signed up with the previous day for a lark. I didn't have any money myself, but I'd created an account using Chloe's credit card, since I'd long ago memorised all the card details from when she used the card in the university café. I had intended to spend a few minutes doing some technical analysis, but I certainly didn't have the patience to draw trend lines and work out Fibonacci retracements right now. In fact, I didn't have the patience for anything much anymore. Glancing at the featured markets, I reckoned that USD/CHF looked ready for a sharp rise, and went long. Then I switched off the laptop, poured my coffee into the grass (as I'd forgotten to drink it, and it was now cold), and walked up and down in the garden for a few minutes longer, pondering what to do next.

It would've been time for me to go to my new part-time job at the local burger place, but I wouldn't be going back there, even as a customer. I'd been fired the previous day for telling my supervisor that he was stupid. It's hard to understand why he fired me, because he actually is exceptionally thick, and I thought I was doing him a favour by pointing this out to him, but he didn't like it. I wasn't even allowed to finish my shift. So I was out of work again, but I didn't mind. I planned to make heaps of money trading the FX markets and playing online poker. Millions of fools played these games, so it shouldn't be too difficult to win.

I decided to have a walk, because pacing up and down in the back garden was not providing me with enough visual stimulation. In T-shirt and shorts, despite the chill wind, I ventured out and walked into Riccarton. Goosebumps formed on my bare arms and the wind rifled through my hair, but I felt truly alive, like every nerve ending in my skin was crying out in joy. I felt more kinaesthetically sensitive than ever before, and it was a deliriously delightful sensation.

I walked quickly, springily, down Riccarton Road and into Hagley Park. A lot of people were out jogging or exercising that morning. I winked at a hot girl in tight track pants and a sweatshirt who was limbering up with some stretches. It's not the sort of thing I've ever done before (the winking), but I did it anyway. Actually—and this was the weird bit—it felt more like I was watching myself do it, like I was sitting in a cinema watching a movie about myself in real time. The girl glared back at me without a word. I laughed loudly and carried on jauntily across the park to the city.

I felt good, really good. I stopped for a coffee and a muffin at a corner café. The woman at the counter was very chatty, and I noticed myself being uncharacteristically talkative in return. She had big tits, only two-thirds concealed by a low-cut blouse. However, she was probably twice my age, so I didn't think about it any further. For some reason I couldn't fathom, but didn't particularly care about either, I was really noticing women at the moment. Sex seemed to be on my mind so much. I would have to do something about my planned special project for the year, and actually try to have some.

After my coffee break, I strode quickly across town to Manchester Street. This is a well-known area for prostitution in the city, an activity that is legal, but I did not see any obvious tarts touting for business at the moment. However, this street also has a concentration of motorcycle shops, and I found myself staring through the windows at some of the sleeker machines on display. I had my face pressed against the window of the Harley-Davidson dealers for so long that one of the salesmen came out to talk to me. I told him that I really fancied a hot set of wheels like one of the touring bikes in the window, but I did not have a motorcycle licence. He laughed and said his customers were usually middle-aged men seeking thrills, and that he would see me again in twenty-five years when I could afford one of the giant mechanical beasts. He directed me to a shop nearby that sold scooters.

By now I quite liked the idea of having a motorbike of any kind, even a little putt-putt scooter. These can be supremely cool, and, well, I'm feeling pretty cool nowadays.

They had a wide selection, but the salesman told me that I could only ride a 50cc model on the kind of driving licence I had. I paced up and down in the store thinking about this. The image of myself stealing a scooter and crashing through the double-glazed window on one wheel came to mind, and I grinned impishly.

Impulsively, I decided to buy a little green Italian-styled model. Again, Chloe's credit card came in useful, because I had no way of paying for this myself with my own funds. There seemed to be an interminable amount of paperwork before I could take it away, but I chatted merrily to the salesman while filling this out, talking man-things such as bikes and chicks and so on.

Eventually, though, I strapped on the helmet I had also bought (and which Chloe had unknowingly paid for) and pushed my new green machine out of the shop onto the road. Confidently stepping across it, I pressed the 'on' button and skidded off down the street with glee, the wind whipping the loose sleeves of my T-shirt. I felt chilled but so full of vitality, and quickly got the hang of the scooter and the measure of its capabilities, which were somewhat less than those of the Harley-Davidson models I had admired earlier, but it was still a lot of fun.

I accelerated across town, surfing orange lights on the one-way system, then did a couple of circuits of the four avenues. By now I was chilled to the bone, but I didn't mind. It started raining lightly. The cold raindrops beat on my bare arms like hundreds of tiny slivers of ice, and I laughed out loud at the sensation. Shit, if rain felt this good, what would sex feel like? I could hardly wait to find out.

Some kids in a car next to me at the traffic lights pointed and giggled, seeing my laughter. I gave them the finger and that shut them up. Or, rather, it seemed as if I was watching myself give them the finger. It's not something I've done before. But now I felt I was capable of anything. Nothing was out of my reach now. And everything I did felt that it was all right. It just didn't matter what the consequences would be, as I couldn't be bothered thinking about them.

I tore down Riccarton Road towards home with the scooter whining like a cheap hair dryer on overdrive. The traffic on that road was, as usual, pretty busy, but being on a scooter I reasoned that normal road rules did not apply to me, and I did not have to wait in line with the other traffic. I weaved amongst stationary and slowly-moving cars, and powered up the inside. At one point, I almost had an accident as a car that I hadn't seen turned from the other side of the road right across me, but the driver saw me and stopped. The blare of its horn faded into the distance behind me as I continued speedily on my way. Before long, I was at home.

My clothes were soaked from the rain, so I left my shoes and socks in the hallway and discarded my T-shirt, shorts and sodden underwear on the kitchen floor. The euphoria of my first scooter ride, albeit in the rain, was dying down a little. I resumed pacing up and down in the living room, having forgotten to go upstairs to put on dry clothes. I knew I should probably get something to eat, because it was almost dinner time, but I just couldn't even concentrate on that. Instead, I padded up and down on bare feet with nothing on, contemplating the global economic crisis and talking into a digital voice tracer that I usually use for university tutorials.

I didn't even hear the front door open and close. The first I knew that Stef was home was when I saw her in the living room doorway, staring at me with a wide-eyed expression.

"Robert! What are you doing?" she demanded.

I paused in mid-stride and mid-sentence. "I'm dictating a document to the Chairman of the Federal Reserve," I said. "The US shouldn't embark on another round of quantitative easing. QE is not to be. Easing is not pleasing."

"And you're doing this in the nude?"

"It's not a video conference, Stef. He won't know what I show. He won't care that I'm bare."

Slowly, she put her handbag down on the sofa. "Are you all right, Robert?"

"I feel freakin' fantastic. I've so much energy. Everything feels good."

"Whose is that scooter in the driveway?" she asked suddenly.

"Mine. I just bought it. It's really cool. I just had to have it."

"I didn't think you could afford anything like that."

"No? Well, I found some money, honey. Now I have to get on with this letter, Stef. It can't wait, it can't be late. I must email it tonight. I expect they'll want me to fly over later in the week to explain my theories to them. You'll tell Chloe where I've gone, won't you?"

"You're talking differently. Faster. You're rhyming, and you're almost babbling," said Stef slowly, as if to emphasise the difference.

I'd realised that, but it didn't actually feel like it was me talking. It felt like I was listening to myself say things that I wouldn't normally say, in a way I wouldn't normally say them. This was extremely strange, but somehow I didn't mind at all.

"I'm more confident now. The second anti-depressant pill has finally taken effect. I feel just amazing."

"And what are you going to do after you've sent your

letter to the Chairman of the Federal Reserve or whoever?" said Stef in a strange voice.

"I don't know. Maybe an assignment, or maybe have another ride on my new scooter. Or maybe cruise some bars picking up hot chicks for casual sex."

Stef curled one side of her mouth down in a way similar to when she discovers the milk in the refrigerator has gone off, or one of her ex-boyfriends calls on the phone.

"Get yourself dressed, Robert," she said. She turned away and went upstairs.

Chapter Eight

Books read lately:
Started seventeen books on a variety of subjects, but unable to get into any of them, and abandoned them all.
Number of sexual encounters:
There's bound to be one soon!

I can't bear to watch the television news. Or war documentaries. Or movies like 'Titanic'. They are too intense, too upsetting, an assault and battery on the feeling cognisance. It is simply too much negative emotion for me to process all at once; it floods my senses and sits on my mind like a bloated, malevolent ghost waiting to pounce. Even newspapers have this effect of leaving me feeling low and fearful, so I dare not peruse them, least I catch sight of a headline of some disaster or other.

When others are upset, I am upset too, but I do not know why. When others shout or become angry, I become afraid, fearing attack. A television, switched on, can push uncomfortable and unwelcome experiences into the very environment in which I need to feel safe and calm, my home, so I do not watch it. A friend crying shatters me like an ice pick smashing the surface of a frozen lake. To cope with these onslaughts if they catch me unawares, I pull back, I turn away, I put my head behind a cushion on the sofa, I ignore the pain of others because I cannot face struggling to share it with them; I would lose myself completely and drown in those watery emotions. I withdraw. I sit in the corner and rock slowly until the bad things go away.

Some people say ASD is 'an empathy disorder'. We are unfeeling and uncaring, according to them. But how can they know my inner mind any more than I can know theirs? Sometimes, there is just too much sensation, extremes of emotion beyond the comfortable parameters within which I can operate. Sometimes, the world is simply too intense, the emotions overwhelming, and I withdraw. I have to. But this apparent coldness is not a lack of empathy and feeling; it is a hypersensitivity. It is feeling too much.

I slept fitfully but woke early, bubbling over with an excess of energy. I tried to work some of this off by going out for a run before breakfast, making a circuit of the roads surrounding Addington Raceway, but I felt no less energetic upon my return. Stef had already gone to work by this point. Again I had the house to myself. Chloe would probably not be home until Sunday, two days hence.

After toast and coffee, and more agitated pacing (in the kitchen this time), I sat down at the kitchen table with my laptop and updated my status on Facebook to say that I felt really energised and content with life at present, and did any of my friends know of a SWF looking for a relationship? After posting this, I clicked the 'like' button. I would have clicked the 'love' button, but there isn't one.

I checked on my USD/CHF trade, but it hadn't changed much. Bored with that, and having finished my toast, I found my way back to Chloe's *hatelist.net*. Today it was titled 'that isle'. I thought for a moment and put the burger place supervisor's name on my permanent *hate list*. If only these people could fry in hell. With onions.

Glancing at the clock, I realised that I had to get going swiftly as I had an appointment with Doctor Meg in thirteen minutes. This wasn't for anything important. It was just a routine follow-up since I'd started the anti-depressants. I hurried outside and raced off on my new scooter to the medical centre, where I rode it up onto the footpath and parked it right next to the front door.

There were several elderly people in the waiting room, nodding off while reading issues of *Women's Weekly* or *Vanity Fair* that were at least ten years old. The magazines did not appeal to me, and nor did sitting down, so I paced back and forth in front of the reception. The receptionist glared at me, but I didn't care.

Doctor Meg called me into her office three minutes late. Her shoulder-length blonde hair brushed the collar of her loose turquoise blouse, and for the first time, I noticed how truly gorgeous she was. I sat down and smiled broadly at her.

"You look happy," she said, returning my smile.

"I feel utterly incredible," I said. "I doubled my dose of the anti-depressants to two pills a day nineteen days ago. You said that'd be all right, so I did it. And I feel so much better that I just can't believe it. I feel like I'm exploding with the *joie de vivre*. I'll need another prescription sooner, though."

"Okay. Well, you're certainly sounding better, too. Congratulations." Her voice sounded sweet and kind to me.

"It's all thanks to you. Before this, I was living in the dark, in a social fog. I feel like I'm really alive now. I feel incredible, fantastic, even. You're an amazing woman, you know."

"Pardon?" Her eyes opened wider.

"I mean it. I know that you're married and all, but if things were different, I would want to get to know you better and have a relationship with you. You're a remarkable person: highly intelligent, caring, attractive, fun."

"You shouldn't talk to me like that. It's inappropriate. You're making me very uncomfortable."

"I'm only talking theoretically. If things were different. I just mean to say something complimentary. I'm not being suggestive."

Doctor Meg swivelled her chair back to face the desk, then turned sideways to look at me as she spoke. "I understand, and I take it as a compliment, but even so..."

"You're a true friend to me, Doctor Meg. You've helped me so much, and I can talk to you about anything."

"You're making me feel very uncomfortable, Robert," she repeated, then turned her attention to shuffling some papers at the edge of her desk.

"Well, I want to be honest. It would be wrong for me to be secretive, wouldn't it?"

"It would have been all right if you hadn't said anything."

"Why? That'd be like lying, and it wouldn't change anything."

Doctor Meg pursed her lips, rocked back in her chair and swivelled it round to face me again. "Robert, you're going to have to see another doctor from now on. I can't see you anymore. Ethics, you know."

"No, I don't know. I don't understand. What have I done wrong?"

"This is a professional relationship, not a personal one." She drummed her fingers on the desk. Was she stimming? I wondered, but I did not think that she was.

"But to me, it's personal. I'm the person. You might see hundreds of patients, but I only see one doctor. It's personal to me. I don't know if I can speak to any other doctors. I don't know them."

"You'll have to see another doctor, Robert. It's for your own protection. Now it's time for you to go." She stood up and pointed towards the door.

Somewhat stunned, I left the medical centre and went home.

I paced up and down a lot in the living room, walking several kilometres probably, then ate something sugary for lunch, and I soon felt better. Perhaps I could ask Chloe who her doctor is and go to see her for my prescriptions. I was so pleased that the depression had totally gone now, and I felt as I thought ordinary people do. I was still amazed that ordinary people felt like this all the time. But how did they ever get anything done thinking about sex all the time? And all that pacing. Though maybe I had more energy than most people. I was certainly far more intelligent, and I felt fitter than most. And the social awkwardness that I was used to because of the Asperger's Syndrome seemed to have disappeared as well. I was just surprised that no women had seized me for their sexual pleasure, one at a time or even as a group. Perhaps it was just a matter of time. I certainly hoped that I wouldn't have to wait long.

I spent the rest of the day out walking, trying to get rid of some of the excess energy I had, but I passed most of the time eyeing attractive women. Eventually, though, I came to a fancy menswear shop in Westfield Mall. Immediately, I realised that I would need superior apparel for when I get summoned to New York to expound upon my economic theories to the Federal Reserve, which ought to happen quite soon, so I needed to buy some decent clothes urgently.

I rushed into the shop and spotted a sales assistant,

who had been busy with another customer, but had just become available. I told him what I needed and what I needed it for, and was quickly fitted with a smart black suit. I did not have the patience to try on anything else, but as this fitted, I bought it. With Chloe's credit card number, of course. I talked to the salesman for ten minutes first, or, rather, I heard myself talking to him about all kinds of nonsense. I don't actually know what got into me at that time. He politely listened, though, then sold me the suit. I didn't know that they cost so much.

I bought a coffee at one of the cafés on the concourse and paid for it with a twenty dollar note as I had nothing smaller, and told the delighted counter staff that they could keep the change as a tip. The funny thing is that I couldn't even finish the coffee as I felt so restless, twitching and kicking my feet under the table. I noticed some of the other customers watching me. I wondered if they thought I was handsome. I didn't fancy any of them, though, and, besides, I felt too fidgety to stay there for long.

I walked around the park, carrying the bag with my new suit in it, and then went home. Stef was there and had cooked a stir-fry for herself and Jeff. She invited me to join them for dinner, so I did. I took the opportunity to tell Stef and Jeff more about historonomics. Shit, it's remarkable how stupid and even criminal some of these economists and statesmen were in the old days, blowing up asset bubbles and engaging in fraud or embezzlement on a grand scale. Especially in France. Stef and Jeff must have been terribly interested because they hardly said anything for a while, yet immediately after dinner they excused themselves and went upstairs. Probably to make love, I expect.

I needed to get out. The house felt claustrophobic to me all of a sudden. I mounted my scooter and roared away, racing down Matipo Street towards the racecourse, then on and on towards the Port Hills, several minutes away, even at the scooter's top speed of almost 50kph. Ascending the hills was a bit of a struggle for my little 50cc Italian-styled scooter, but it must have looked cool, even though it was slow.

I'd forgotten to put on a coat or jacket, and it was quite cold now in the evenings and already dark. I reached the *Sign of the Takahe* and turned around, coming to a stop with a view of the city below me. The bright lights of Colombo Street, the longest street in Christchurch, stretched away from me into the distance. I could pick out other notable landmarks and main streets lit up in the dark. Idly, I wondered if the prostitutes were out touting for business on Manchester Street and if they were as cold as me.

I shivered with the cold, then groaned with pleasure at the sensation, as it showed that I was truly alive.

After a while, I rode back home. I didn't see Stef or Jeff for the rest of the evening.

I started Saturday morning the same way as Friday—feeling elated and full of energy after a restless night. Chloe's *hatelist.net* website showed 'heat list' as the title. Again I wondered if this was due to her dyslexia. I'd have to ask her when she returned. But before that, I needed to write a letter to the Chancellor of the Exchequer in the UK criticising their woeful economic policies. I hoped they would not invite me over at the same time as the Federal Reserve because I wouldn't be able to make it. However, I was expecting the Federal Reserve Chairman to phone me any day now, seeking my informed opinions.

After emailing these thoughts and criticisms, I took up the latest book I had been reading, *Pretending To Be*

Normal, and opened it to the place I'd marked with my *Star Trek Voyager* bookmark. I'd been finding the book immensely absorbing, but I just couldn't concentrate at the moment, even to read for a few minutes. I had an uncontrollable urge to be moving about, and I paced up and down the living room, which made it even more difficult to read. After a while, I gave up and went outside, deciding to trek westwards along Riccarton Road towards Church Corner, not for any particular reason, but simply because... Well, I didn't know, really. It was just the direction in which I went.

My mind raced faster than my feet, and I never saw the silver car turning the corner. In fact, I hadn't even realised I was crossing the road. The car lightly bumped my right leg as it screeched to a stop. The driver blared his horn at me. I gave him the finger and went on my way. Or, rather, I noticed myself doing that. I'd done it before too, and it felt terrific.

Today was warmer, and I soon broke into a sweat that evaporated as I walked, producing a lovely, refreshing tingling sensation all over my arms and face. I could have walked forever, but I reached Church Corner and turned back. I had no reason to be there, really, just exercising my legs, trying to quiet the restlessness in them.

I walked back and took my scooter out for a ride on the Southern Motorway, laughing as the wind buffeted me and pushed the scooter from side to side. The cross wind meant the scooter could not travel at its top speed, and I was overtaken by many cars as I wobbled about, criss-crossing the line separating the hard shoulder from the main road as I struggled to keep control. Wow, what a ride, though.

I'm not even sure what I did the rest of the afternoon, I felt so distracted. I know I spent some more money. I bought a jacket for Chloe that I hope fits her, as I paid for it with her credit card. You know, credit cards just make it so easy to buy stuff. I hope she likes it. The jacket, that is.

Evening came, and I noticed that Stef was getting ready to go out. That usually involves a lot of time running between her bedroom and the bathroom, alternating outfits, peering into the mirror and doing things to her hair.

"Where are you going, Stef?" I asked eagerly as she passed me in the hall, wearing a long black dress and a green hat. Maybe she was going somewhere fun, and I could go with her.

"Marianne's having a party tonight, Robert," she said, smiling. "I'm going there, meeting up with friends, you know."

"Can I come?"

Stef looked at me with her mouth popped open. "Sure, if you want to, but I thought you didn't like it the last time."

"I'm so much better now, Stef. The anti-depressants are working really well. Will Teena be there?"

"Probably. She usually is. Well, I'm leaving in ten minutes. If you want to get ready, I'll take you."

"Great!"

Twenty-four minutes later Stef was ready, and she drove us there. On the way, I felt 99.9% excited, so totally different to how I had been just a few weeks earlier. I thought, I can do this now. I can mingle with other people. I've got so much energy, and I feel so confident that it's just not a problem anymore. My left foot kept twitching on the journey though. I think maybe I should have done more exercise to release some of this excess energy.

The music was blaring again, but somehow this time the thundering noise did not irritate and unsettle me. Instead, I found myself nodding to the beat as I followed

Stef into the house, and into the kitchen. She made directly for a couple of girls standing against the wall, drinking coke on the rocks.

"Hey, Teena," she said to one of them, a pretty brown-haired girl in a red top and jeans. "This is Robert. Remember I told you about him once? He's finally made it to a party."

The other girl excused herself and moved away, as did Stef, leaving Teena and me alone together. Teena turned her attention to me and smiled, revealing lovely, straight white teeth. "Hey, Robert. Nice to meet you at last. What's a guy like you doing in a place like this? Stef told me that you found the music and people overwhelming last time."

"What did you say?" I asked, pointing at my ear. The music was playing a particularly loud drum section at the moment.

She took my elbow and tilted her head to indicate, I think, that she wanted me to follow her. We went out into the back garden, where it was a little quieter. I could almost hear myself think. And breathe. I think I was panting a little.

"We can talk here," said Teena. "It's not as noisy as inside. And it's not too cold tonight. Stef's told me a lot about you, all good. You sound like an interesting guy. You're studying economics, right?"

"Yes, that's right. I'm really passionate about economics, and the history of economics," I said. Then I remembered that Stef had coached me to ask questions that show an interest in the other person, so I added, "And what do you do?"

"I'm studying economics too. We're probably in the same class, Econ 101."

"Yes, we must be. Maybe we can meet up after the class sometimes, if you're free."

She moved a little closer to me. She was slightly shorter than me, and looked up at me with wide hazelnut coloured eyes. "Most of the guys here are only interested in drinking and talking about sports."

"I'm not like that. I'm different to them."

"So I've heard," she said.

I strained to hear this, because it was just a murmur.

"I really like an intelligent guy who can talk to me about intelligent things," continued Teena.

"Well, I'm highly intelligent, Teena." What was I supposed to say next? Stef had told me to give genuine and spontaneous compliments, so I thought of one that I had planned earlier. "And you seem like a really nice and attractive young woman."

Yes! I thought as she beamed at me. Her teeth reflected the pale white light from the outdoor bulb, which seemed to flicker because of the moths circling it like little moons around a planet on fire.

"Stef tells me that you're honest and direct," she said. Her head was tilted to one side, and her tongue played on her top lip as she gazed at me. "I like that in a guy. A penny for your thoughts?"

"What do you mean, a penny for my thoughts?"

She laughed, then smiled at me. "It's just a saying. Tell me what you're thinking about. We'll talk."

Well, that was easy. She wants me to be direct, so, okay, I'll do that.

"Wanna fuck?"

I never saw her move, but I felt the ice-cold coke splash against my face. It actually felt quite refreshing, in a way. An ice cube struck me on the cheek and bounced off into the grass. I'd closed my eyes as her drink hit me. When I opened them again, she was gone.

I walked home, feeling somewhat less euphoric than in the past few days. My mood seemed to be changing with every step I took in the night, sinking lower and lower like the setting moon. Behind me, the blaring music faded away to nothing, and I concentrated on the soft footfalls of my feet on the pavement. In my head, my conversation with Teena played like a CD on continuous repeat; every word she had said, and every word I had heard myself say.

Chapter Nine

Books read lately:
By the Time You Read This, I'll Be Dead – Julie Anne Peters, and *Prozac Nation* – Elizabeth Wurtzel
Number of sexual encounters:
Absolutely none yet

People with Asperger's do not consider themselves disabled. They consider themselves different.
  If you have met one person with Asperger's...then you have met one person with Asperger's.

I just wanted to die. I lay on the sofa most of Sunday, and those thoughts passed through my mind every few minutes. I just wanted to die, but it was not going to happen to me while I lay there on the sofa. I would have to do something, but I felt listless, completely drained of energy, the absolute polar opposite to the excess of energy I had experienced for the past few days.

Stef looked in on me a few times. She had not said anything to me. Maybe she thought I was ill, and she should keep away in case she caught something horrible. Maybe Teena had told her how I had spoken to her, and Stef felt angry towards me because she thought I was horrid. Which I was, entirely. But she did make me a sandwich at one point. I cannot remember if I ate it or not.

I cannot understand why I spoke to Teena in the way

that I did. It was so uncharacteristic of me. It did not even feel like it was me saying the words. It was, but it felt like I was listening to someone else, as if I was under some kind of spell. Until the magic was broken by ice-cold coke being thrown in my face.

Chloe came home on Sunday evening. She said 'hello' to me, but I did not answer. I kind of did reply in my mind, but the words did not come out of my mouth. She went upstairs without another word and came down again later. I had not changed position, though I was stimming by repeatedly lifting my right arm from the elbow and letting it drop back to the sofa with a dull 'thud'. I had been doing this off and on throughout the day. It grounded me.

I sensed Chloe was watching me. My own eyes were closed. Some of the events of the past few days were passing through my mind like an old 'B' horror movie in which I was the leading character. Or the monster. Maybe even a bit of both.

Then I remembered with some guilt that I had been spending money on Chloe's credit card.

"Are you all right, Robert? 'Cause, really, you don't look all right at all. I've never seen you looking like this. You look completely whacked out," she said.

"No," I managed to say before she continued.

"What's happened? Did you get fired again? Fail a test? No, wait, there're no test results this week. Have you had some bad news from someone? Your mother? What's going on?"

I did not know how to respond to that, so I said nothing. I wished she would shut up and leave me alone.

"Have you been taking your anti-depressants? You better have been, Robert. You can't come off those all of a sudden. It's too much of a shock to the system. I had a friend once who did that, and she was found—"

"I have been taking them," I mumbled, interrupting. "I increased the dose, remember."

"I told you to be careful. Weren't you? There is a reason why these aren't sold over the counter like jelly beans. Why did you increase it?"

I did not answer. I could not remember anymore why I did that.

"Robert, did you feel high for a while?"

At this suggestion, I opened my eyes and turned my head slightly, so I could see Chloe. She was sitting on the other sofa, leaning forward with her hands clasped. She softly tapped her left heel on the floor.

"High?"

"Feeling really good. Confident. Impetuous. Energetic. Restless. Doing and saying stuff you normally wouldn't do. Not acting like yourself. Maybe even feeling like you're super-clever or can't be harmed or something. Feeling like you're watching yourself in a movie do lots of crazy stuff."

"Yes. Pretty much all of that," I said weakly, closing my eyes again and turning to face the back of the sofa.

"Shit," she said, and was silent for so long that I thought she must have gone away without me hearing, for Chloe is seldom short of words. Eventually, she said, "For how long?"

"A few days. Maybe a week. And now I hate myself. I just want to die."

"It'll pass," said Chloe matter-of-factly. "For how long have you been feeling low? A few days? A week? It's important."

"Just today."

"Shit."

I stayed silent and unmoving. I honestly did not know what to say. Chloe seemed to be making me feel worse.

"We've got Uni tomorrow, Robert. Try to get some rest tonight. Tomorrow, keep yourself really busy, so busy that you don't stop to think. And make sure you go to see your doctor. I've got to go to bed now myself. I'm exhausted. Talk to you tomorrow."

I heard her leave the room. I decided to sleep on the sofa. The stairs seemed like too much of an obstacle at the moment.

I slept listlessly.

There is a screaming in my head. It is me, or some part of me that has been woken up like a kraken disturbed from the seabed by a passing ship, surfacing to drag the boat and sailors to a watery grave. With each scream, I feel myself sinking lower and lower into an abyss, dark and suffocating. A voice—my voice—has started up in my mind, telling me how worthless I am, that I am such a pariah no woman will ever notice me, that no one will care if I got hit by a bus. In fact, they will probably not even bother to remove the body, but just leave it there for the birds to pick at and the car wheels to crush into mush.

I was not so lethargic today. I got up from the sofa, but did not bother to change my clothes from the rumpled ones I had slept in. I made some breakfast. Stef made hers quietly at the same time, but took it upstairs to eat, which was unusual. She normally likes to talk during breakfast. Anyway, I was glad she went away. I did not want to listen to her, and I had nothing to say myself.

Chloe had not got up before I left home and walked to the medical centre. It was only as I got there that I remembered I was not allowed to see Doctor Meg anymore. I hesitated at the counter, but it was too late to retreat, for the receptionist was already staring at me and asking me if she could help. I wanted to say 'no' but the appropriate social response in this situation is 'yes', so I said that. She said I could see a Doctor Hee Ling. That would normally have made me laugh, but today I did not feel anything.

Doctor Hee Ling asked me a few questions and poked at my chest a bit, but mostly read over my case notes. I did not feel comfortable with him because I did not know him at all. It takes me a while to feel comfortable with someone when I first meet them. I spent more time looking at his shoes (shiny black ones) than his face (which had a narrow goatee beard).

He asked how the anti-depressants were working, and I mumbled something. I do not remember exactly what I said, or notice whether or not he heard or seemed to understand it. He asked about my eating and sleeping. I said I had not been sleeping much and felt tired. He gave me a script for some Tamazepam, and then I left.

I walked on towards university, deciding to get the sleeping pills later. I do not know why he gave me that prescription. I had not been sleeping much because I had had so much energy, and now that was gone I could sleep properly again. But it was good he offered it to me, as it saved me the trouble of asking. I had already considered that an overdose of sleeping pills might work for me.

While I was walking, I had time to think. It was unstructured time, so the thoughts just rushed in to fill the gap in my head where normally the struggle to interpret everyday life takes place. But now all the rushing thoughts, racing thoughts even, were negative, reminding me that other people ignore me because I am worthless, or, if they notice me, they instantly despise me. I said nothing to anyone who said 'hello' to me, but I talked to myself. I said 'I hate myself' and 'I just want to die'. It seemed right somehow to vocalise it, as if hearing myself say it out loud validated it and made it even more real.

I reached university and attended a lecture. I had already missed one, but Chloe had told me to keep myself occupied, so I went to the next. I could not concentrate, though. I looked at all the people around me, scribbling furiously or laughing quietly amongst themselves. I wondered if they were writing about me, laughing about me. That would not be rational, however. I was nothing to them.

After a while, I walked out of the lecture and strolled aimlessly around the campus. Idly, I wondered how long it would take for someone leaping from the top of the library to hit the ground. Even accelerating at almost ten metres per second per second it would still take some time. I wondered if I would scream or feel it when I hit. But I did not like that thought. That was a terribly disagreeable thought. Very distressing.

I left university mid-afternoon, deciding to skip my last lecture, and walked home slowly, calling in at the pharmacy on the way to pick up the prescription and buy three packets of Paracetamol. I kicked at the ground as I walked, thinking how stupid I was to have bought a scooter I could not afford, and then not even ride it to university. I wondered how fast it could go on the open road (probably not particularly fast, I guessed), and how many trucks would come by on the other side. I would only need one large one, of course.

I thought about a lot of things that I should not have been thinking about. I kind of knew this was wrong, that it must be absurd to think like this...but it strangely felt quite reasonable. Who would miss me if I was not here? I asked myself. My mother? Hardly. Chloe? Stef? For a few days, maybe. While, if I hung around in the world—into which I fit as poorly as an ugly crone's foot into a glass slipper—there would just be more pain and loneliness in store for me. Surely, the sensible thing was to put an end to it sooner rather than later?

The black mist in my mind had lifted a little when I reached home. Maybe because the walking produced endorphins or something like that. I did not know. I put my paper bag from the pharmacy on the kitchen table and went to sit on one of the sofas in the living room, staring at a point on the floor (which was carpeted and included a variety of food and drink stains garnered over many years), tapping my left foot and sometimes scratching my left ear.

After some time (I do not know how long), I heard the front door open and close. Five seconds later, Chloe strode into the living room. She stopped and stared at me. I stared expressionlessly back at her. She was wearing tight jeans and a blue sleeveless top (because it was a Monday).

"I missed you in the café today," she remonstrated. "I waited an hour and a half. You never showed up."

"Sorry," I said. I had utterly forgotten this.

"Never mind, I worked on an assignment. A psychology one. Almost the same as one I did last year, so it didn't take long. Then I started rereading *Aspergirls*. And I had two green teas because you weren't there to talk to. Are you still feeling low, Robert?"

I nodded, staring into her seemingly bottomless eyes. For an Aspie, she was quite perceptive sometimes.

"Did you see your doctor? Meg, isn't it? Did you tell her about this? About increasing your dose of anti-depressants? You'll need to step it down under her guidance. It's the only safe way."

"She will not see me anymore. I did not feel like talking to the new doctor. I do not know him. He gave me some sleeping pills, though."

"Sleeping pills? What? Where are they?"

"On the kitchen table."

Chloe rushed out and returned mere seconds later with the pharmacy bag. She withdrew a plastic bottle from it and held it up right in front of my face as I sat unmoving on the sofa. She held it so close that I got a shock and stopped tapping my left foot.

"Tamazepam!" she shouted. "What do you want this for?"

I shrugged. Was it not obvious?

"Jesus, Robert. What else have you got in here?" She up-ended the paper bag onto the other sofa. Three packets of Paracetamol fell out and bounced lightly on the cushioned seats. She dropped the empty bag and grabbed the Paracetamol in her left hand. "What the fuck's this, Robert?"

"Paracetamol," I said wearily.

"Sixty of them? Jesus, Robert. You shouldn't have any more than eight of these in the house at any one time. Now, just sit there. I'm getting rid of all this shit."

She marched out. I heard her stomping up the stairs. A minute later, I heard the toilet flush, and then I heard her coming down again. In one small part of my mind, I knew she was right, that she was looking after me, caring for me. Somehow, that made me feel a little bit better, so I do not know why I started crying. At first it was just some quiet sobs. Then I buried my head in my hands, and I could not stop. A kind of barking, coughing cry came out, like that of a wounded animal.

I sensed Chloe sit down on my right. She put her arm around my shoulders and pulled me to her. I turned to her and cried into her bare neck and shoulder, the tears cascading down my face onto her skin.

After a while, I sat up and was silent for a few moments.

"When I was high—out of control—I bought a scooter using your credit card number," I confessed. "And other stuff. I did not really think about it much at the time. I am sorry."

"That's what it's like. Crazy things happen." She ran her fingers through her hair, flicking it. "Did you have to use my credit card? Well, I suppose you didn't have any money, did you?"

I shook my head.

"Where's the scooter?" she asked suddenly.

"Outside, by the gate."

"No," she said slowly. "It's definitely not there. I would have seen it when I came in. Actually, I remember seeing it last night, but it's certainly not there now."

I looked into her eyes sorrowfully.

"Insurance?" she asked, but immediately answered her own question. "Of course not. You were in no state to think of that. Shit. It's been stolen, and you haven't got any insurance. And you paid for it on my credit card! Jesus, Robert!"

I started to feel low again. Not only were the options with the pills unavailable now, riding the scooter into a truck was also not viable any longer.

"Let's sort you out," declared Chloe. "Now, why did Meg say she couldn't see you anymore? Is she moving overseas or something?"

"No, I said I liked her. She said something about ethics and protection and stuff."

"Fucking bitch. She sent you away just when you needed her the most, when things were going crazy. I'll phone her. What's the number?"

I told her. She dialled it, and started spinning a pen in her left hand while she waited for the receptionist to pick up.

"Hello? I'm calling about my friend, Robert Barnes. He's very ill. I need to speak to his doctor, Meg something, right away." Pause. "I know he saw another doctor, and he got prescribed Tamazepam, which I've just flushed down the loo. It's Meg who knows all about him. She's been seeing him for years." Pause. "Look, put me through to her, or I'll come down to the Medical Centre, and we'll have this conversation in the waiting room in front of everyone." Pause.

Chloe stopped spinning her pen and leaned against the wall, looking at me with a little smile upon her lips. She mouthed something which I could not understand because I do not lip-read.

"Meg? My name's Chloe Wilson. I'm a friend of your patient Robert Barnes. He's very ill. I need to speak to you about him." Pause. "Wait—I'll put you on speaker-phone, so Robert can hear you. He's right here. What did you say?"

Doctor Meg's disembodied voice, rendered somewhat harsh and metallic by the cheap phone, echoed around the room. "I said, he's not my patient anymore, and I cannot discuss a patient with anyone else anyway."

"He gives his consent to you discussing him with me," said Chloe. "Don't you, Robert?" She held the phone over to me briefly, and I said 'yes', then sat down on the front edge of the sofa to listen to the two of them.

"That doesn't change anything. He's still not my patient anymore. It was a question of ethics."

"Ethics? What do you mean, ethics? He's very ill and needs to be seen right away! Isn't his health and well-being the most important ethical consideration?"

"Look," stuck on Meg bravely in the face of Chloe's outburst, "it's not a personal relationship. It's a professional relationship. He crossed the boundary. I can't see him anymore."

"Well, it's personal to him. You held his life in your hands, in your mind. How could it be more personal than that?"

A sigh came through the telephone, amplified because Chloe had stabbed at the volume button with her finger and turned it up. It sounded like a tornado ripping up a tin roof. "What's the matter with him?"

"Extreme mood instability. He increased his dosage of the anti-depressants and had a hypomanic episode. Now he's depressed and at risk."

"Increasing the dosage shouldn't have made any difference."

"It can do, sometimes," declared Chloe.

She had her left fist clenched so tightly the knuckles were white. I thought she was going to hit something. Possibly Doctor Meg if she had been in the room with us. Chloe's right hand gripped the receiver so hard I would not have been surprised to see it snap in half. I stayed on the sofa, unmoving, watching and listening intently.

"You know something about this, do you, Chloe?"

"Yes. A lot, actually. The SSRIs can induce hypomania, but there's also a possibility that Robert is bipolar. I have a friend who's bipolar, and I'm suspected bipolar and on mood stabilisers, so I know something about that. I don't think Robert is bipolar, though. I think it's a reaction to the anti-depressants."

"Did you say you think he is at risk?"

"Yes. He's clearly very low. He bought five dozen Paracetamol too, which I've disposed of. He needs his medication reduced. He needs to be monitored."

"Then take him to Psych. Emergency."

"No, I'll stay with him. But I want you to see him tomorrow morning, doctor."

"No, I won't. I can't. Ethics."

There was a click. Doctor Meg had hung up.

A little while later, Stef came home from work. I overheard Chloe talking to her, telling her what had happened to me. I kind of understood it by then, so I stopped listening after a while.

Instead, I tried to remember which pair of ribs a knife has to bisect in order to penetrate the heart. Was it the third and fourth? Or the fourth and fifth? Or a different pair altogether? I could go and look it up on the internet, but if Chloe saw me doing that, she would not let me get a knife…so I should get the knife from the kitchen first…but then she will wonder why I am sitting at my laptop with a knife. I gave a faint groan. At the moment, I could not even make a simple decision like that.

The moment passed. Chloe came and turned on the TV and sat with me while Stef heated up some of last night's stir-fry remains for our dinner. Chloe and Stef talked about mundane things while we ate, but I said nothing. I noticed that Chloe had not given me a knife to eat my dinner with. Would a fork work? I wondered. I decided it was too bendy to be effective as a stabbing instrument and would probably just get tangled up in my ribs.

Chloe followed me around the house all evening like a shadow. I grew weary of it, but she did not seem to mind. When it was time to go to bed, she dragged the mattress from her room into mine and slept on it there. I slept fitfully in my bed. I had nightmares of demons chasing me with knives, but somehow I always managed to elude them.

Morning came. When I woke, I saw Chloe sitting on the end of my bed, watching me. She had changed into her (Tuesday) black sleeveless top. The mattress on the floor had been taken away.

"Are you feeling any better today, Robert?" she asked immediately.

"I hate myself," I said with conviction.

Chloe nodded. "I thought so."

I showered and got dressed while Chloe fixed up breakfast for us of eggs and toast. For a while, I wondered how many people committed suicide by choking themselves on scrambled eggs. Probably not many, I reasoned.

Stef came into the kitchen, hurrying, as usual, to get ready for work. She normally gave herself four minutes to have breakfast, sometimes five. Today, she stretched it out to seven minutes by asking me how I was.

"I wish I was dead," I said, but I had begun to wonder if that would work. With my luck, I would probably come back as some kind of ghost or zombie or something. Or maybe there actually is life after death. That would be a cruel trick.

"Robert, I know you've been affected by your medication, and it's not your fault," said Stef between spoonfuls of cornflakes, "but do try to cheer up a bit. You've got a lot to look forward to, you know. Like riding your new scooter—"

"It was stolen."

"Well, er…um…"

I waited. Silence fell. I broke it by tapping my foot on the tiled floor.

"What I'm saying is, don't let yourself get down, Robert. Life's too short for that."

"It is not short enough," I retorted.

"He's not 'letting himself get down'," corrected Chloe. "It's a chemical reaction to the SSRIs."

"Whatever," said Stef. She rolled her eyes, a motion I could not interpret yet, and left the room.

The phone rang. I stopped my foot tapping. Chloe grabbed the phone. "Yes?" she said, listened for a moment, then put it onto speaker-phone.

"Doctor Meg? What were you saying? You're on speaker-phone now. Robert's here, and he can hear you."

"I said, bring him in. He needs caring for."

"You said you couldn't see him because of ethics."

"Screw them. I've changed my mind. Robert's my patient. I'll make him well."

Chapter Ten

Books read lately:
None... Could not concentrate to read
Number of sexual encounters:
Still none, nil, zero, not a sausage...

I am not an incomplete jigsaw who needs solving, fixing or curing... I am just put together in a different way. Who is to say what the final picture should look like anyway? Some might say I am not normal, but more accurately, I could say that I am not typical. I perceive and experience life through the filter of ASD. But NS people perceive and experience life through filters, too... It is just that their filters are more prevalent than mine, that they think the way they see things is the 'correct' way, though it is simply the most common.
 I am not odd... Just different.
 Celebrate and accept neurodiversity.

Doctor Meg was true to her word. She saw me that morning, with Chloe in attendance, got me to reduce my medication to one pill a day, and write down in a notebook how I felt from day to day (even hour to hour if I was particularly volatile, using a thick red or black marker pen to express vividly how extreme I felt). She instructed me to come back to see her every two days until I felt better. I was immensely grateful to her.

 In the next few days, I missed most of my classes at

university, the first week of the second term. I was emotional at times, unable to focus on anything, and simply did not feel up to going to lectures, as I would not have been able to pay attention. I did almost nothing, apart from walk and rest. Even reading a book was beyond me.

Chloe missed most of her classes too, though we managed to go to Econ 101 together. She barely left my side for those difficult days, and continued to drag her mattress into my room at night to sleep on the floor next to my bed. She said she was a light sleeper and would wake instantly if I tried to leave the room. I did not mind her continual presence, though. I knew she was looking after me, making sure I was safe, talking to me, encouraging me through the darkest and bleakest patches of those almost intolerable days and nights. My constant unofficial 'therapist'.

By the time two weeks had passed, I felt very good. I cannot say I felt 'normal', because I do not know what 'normal' is. And by 'very good', I do not mean that I felt super-confident and high as a kite. I meant that I felt stable, relaxed and calm like never before. There were no dreadful thoughts in my head and no crazy impulses either. I had plateaued at the right level at last. And for the first ever time, I felt truly free—free of the shadows in my head that had plagued me for years, free of the self-critical voice, free of self-hate. In complete control of myself and my life. I had a sense of calm that I knew would raise my self-confidence like fertiliser feeding a starving vine that wants to climb into the light and embrace everything it can reach.

Chloe did not want to drop out of university for a second year in a row, so we doubled our efforts to catch up on missed lectures and study. Doctor Meg furnished us with medical certificates to hand in with our late assignments. We worked late into the night, every night. Stef helped us out by cooking meals and doing all the housework and shopping chores. Chloe had to cease working on her web app in the interim too, such was her determination to regain lost study time, and I did not read as avariciously as I usually did. But we managed it. We copied all the lecture notes from other students, read the relevant passages in the textbooks and started to hand assignments in on time again. We caught up.

We decided to celebrate by going out for dinner to a restaurant in Upper Riccarton, which was a pleasant walking distance for us of about half an hour. The evening was cool and dry. We asked Stef and Jeff (who had come over to see her) if they wanted to join us, but they declined, saying they had other plans for celebrating during the evening. So Chloe and I set off by ourselves.

I was used to feeling virtually invisible to the world whenever I went anywhere by myself, as my everyday clothes and unremarkable appearance gave no one any reason to glance at me more than momentarily, if at all. Usually I would find myself having to step aside while oncoming pedestrians never deviated a centimetre from their intended path, and would have walked straight into me as if I did not exist for them.

This phenomenon was, if anything, worse when I was out with Chloe, because Chloe attracted everyone's attention. She was slim, strikingly beautiful with the unconventional appearance of dyed cobalt blue hair and facial piercings. Men and women alike would turn, agape, to look at Chloe, and seem to be totally unaware of me, and, indeed, anything else. I often had to duck and dive around star-struck pedestrians while Chloe simply marched on relentlessly, sucking attention like a black hole sucks in stars.

However, all this had changed since Doctor Meg had made me properly well. I strode alongside Chloe with a sense of greater confidence and composure. Oncoming pedestrians side-stepped us to the same degree that I made way for them. Sometimes they even smiled at me. I was truly in a different world now. A world that, though it did not embrace me, did not shun me either.

A world in which I suddenly remembered that I had left my wallet at home. I had intended to pay for our meal with the last of the money I had earned from the temporary part-time jobs at which I had worked. I had put my wallet in my jacket pocket, and then, when leaving home, decided not to bring the jacket, as it did not seem cool enough for me to require it.

"Chloe. I have to go back and get my wallet. I left it in my jacket on the sofa."

Chloe stopped walking and turned to face me. "Okay. I'll go on to the restaurant. It's usually very busy there. It's ninety-five percent likely that we'll have to wait for a table anyway. I'll get us put on the waiting list and go to the bar. It's usually not too loud for me, so I'm sure you'll be okay there. I can get us a couple of drinks. You know what I mean, one drink each. How long do you think you'll be?"

I glanced at my watch to determine exactly how long we had been walking, doubled it and added a couple of minutes. "I will be about twenty-four minutes behind you."

"Cool. See you there."

We separated, Chloe going on while I turned back. I walked home, sensing the same feeling of self-assuredness that I had felt walking with her. There was a little bounce in my step. My stride was longer than it used to be. My head was held up, rather than bent over perusing the cracks and lines of the pavement. For the first time in my life, I was just happy with being myself.

I reached home, opened the front door and went

inside. It should only take me a minute to fetch my jacket. Maybe I would not be as far behind Chloe as I had guessed, perhaps only twenty-two minutes.

I was just pondering whether to text her to let her know that I might be two minutes faster than I had said, when I became aware of some unusual sounds emanating from the living room, like someone exercising vigorously, and that was odd, because I knew that Stef did not exercise at all.

I reached the living room in four seconds. My jacket was lying over the arm of one of the sofas, where I had left it, but it was what was happening on the other sofa that caught my attention. I could see Jeff's head at the near end, bobbing up and down as he lay on his back, his feet stretched out to the far end. Stef was sitting astride him, her white blouse loose and pulled up a little, with Jeff's hands inside. She was rising up and down rhythmically, one hand clenching the back of the sofa for support, her eyes opening and closing and gasping for breath.

"Oh...God...Oh...God...Oh...God...Oh...Shit!"

When she saw me, she sat back with a look of surprise, smoothing out her clothes as Jeff's hands dropped away. She grabbed a couple of cushions to cover herself and Jeff, who had wriggled his legs out from under her and swung them down to the floor. I heard the sound of a zip and a gasp of pain.

"How long have you been there, Robert?" asked Stef, her mouth wide-open as she wriggled back behind one of the cushions and wiped the sweat from her brow with her left hand.

"Just a few seconds. I returned to get my wallet. It is in the pocket of my jacket there." I pointed, and she looked. "Sorry for interrupting. Were you having sex?"

Stef flushed red, probably with the exertion she appeared to have been under. Jeff got unsteadily to his feet and stared at me with an expression I recognised as anger. That one is usually easy to spot. Instinctively, I looked away and down to the floor, unable to return his gaze.

"What sort of fucking stupid question is that?" he snapped. "Why didn't you just turn around and walk away, Bob? Are you a pervert or something?"

"Jeff, calm down—" started Stef.

"My name is Robert," I said, concentrating intently on the floor.

"Well, *Robert*, how would you like being interrupted during sex?"

"I do not know." That is, of course, true. I had no idea. It had not happened to me yet, either the sex or any interruption during it.

"You don't know? Are you a fucking retard or something? Look at me when I'm talking to you!"

"Jeff, stop it!" protested Stef, standing up and grabbing his arm. "You're scaring him. It's not his fault. He can't look at you and listen to you at the same time with all your carrying on."

Jeff shook her off. Out of the corner of my eye, I could see him advancing towards me. I remained silent. I could sense feelings of panic starting to roll around in my head, making it spin. I heard the voice of my childhood invisible friend, Sam, in my head, telling me, '*Get out of there!*' This time, I did not move.

He pushed me so hard in the chest that it took my breath away. I fell backwards against the door frame, then tumbled onto the floor in the doorway. Before I could get up, Jeff kicked me in the leg with a socked foot. It did not hurt much. I scrambled to my feet, unsure of what was coming next, and undecided as to whether to run or stay. If I ran, would Stef be safe with this man who seemed to have completely lost control?

Jeff had moved to the other sofa and picked up my jacket, which he now flung at me. "Take this and fuck off." He turned back towards Stef with a grin, as if I had already left, and he had forgotten me.

His grin disappeared as she slapped him hard on the left side of his face.

"You don't talk to my friends like that!" she shouted. "Now piss off yourself. This relationship is over."

Pausing only to swoop down to pick up Jeff's discarded shoes and then shove them hard into his stomach, she turned him around and virtually frogmarched him out of the living room. I hastily stepped out of the way into the hall. Jeff offered no resistance or said anything, but he shook his head a lot. Stef shoved him out of the front door and slammed it closed behind him. Then she turned to me.

"Sorry, Robert," she said. Her blouse was hanging down over the top part of her thighs, but she didn't have her jeans on, or any shoes. "I suspected he was a creep, and now I know it."

I became aware of a pain in my shoulder blade where it had hit the door frame. I did not know what to say. Stef seemed to be waiting for an answer.

"Sorry, Stef," I said, though immediately I wondered what I was being apologetic about.

"It's not your fault, Robert. And I'm better off without him anyway, now that I know he can be like that. It's better to lose a lover, than to love a loser."

I could not comment on that from experience, so I just

smiled at her instead.

"Give me five minutes," she said. "I'll join you and Chloe for dinner. We'll take my car. And I'm paying."

Chapter Eleven

Books read lately:
Where Are the Customers' Yachts? – Fred Schwed (note: this is not querying the whereabouts of some millionaires' ocean playthings; it is a self-described 'good hard look at Wall Street', in particular the financial madness of the 1920s...)
Number of sexual encounters:
None... Will this ever change?

Attn: Robert Barnes
   From: An outsourced public relations office somewhere in Asia, on behalf of the Federal Reserve
   Subject: Your recent submission highlighting the alleged malpractices and wayward policies of our office
   Dear Mr Barnes
   Thank you most kindly for your recent letter, which we have duly considered and filed in the appropriate file, in which no one will ever see it again. I am advised to inform you most sincerely that your offered services are not required by the most humble office of the Federal Reserve. We are not going to fly you to our offices by Concorde to listen to your views. For your kind information, Concorde no longer operates, in any case, regardless of your intended travel plans and lecture tour.
   Your views on inflation and depression were of interest to us, but only from the point of view that they differed so

markedly from the policies and direction we are most certainly taking for the future well-being of our citizens, by which I mean the citizens of the country to which we are contracted to provide our stellar public relations service. I am also advised to advise you that it would be inadvisable of you to write to our office again regarding this matter. Your name has been added to a secret list for this very purpose.

We hope most kindly that our considered missive deals with your issue most thoroughly and to your utmost satisfaction. Irrespective of this, we consider this issue closed.

The Federal Reserve, as part of its service to the American people, the world as a whole and, indeed, the shaky structure that is our global financial system, has decided to trial a variation of quantitative easing (QE). You have been randomly selected. Please find, pinned to this letter, $250 (two hundred and fifty dollars) of brand new, printed money. We have printed the new money on recycled paper to keep costs down and to save the environment. Please spend it and borrow more.

A few days later, I was playing around with Chloe's website *hatelist.net* again. The title had recently changed from 'his latte' to 'halt ties'. Some of the anagrams the site was coming up with were actually rather curious, I thought.

I had just finished adding a number of political leaders and renowned economists to my permanent *hate list*, along with Stef's ex-boyfriend Jeff, when I noticed that Chloe had created a 'send poison pen email' function, and I made use of that. I do not know what it did, if anything, but it sure made me feel better, even if it did not make the political leaders, economists and Jeff feel any worse.

I shut down my laptop, which I had been using at the

kitchen table, and sat quietly for nine minutes, stimming by twitching my left foot against the chair leg. While I sat there, I tried to decide what to do next. I had abandoned my comprehensive daily timetables some weeks before as I had found them more effort to keep to than they were worth. I think they helped more when I was suffering from depression and not thinking clearly. I still did not like unstructured time, though.

I got up, thinking that I might go for a long walk, but at that moment Chloe came into the house carrying a large cuboid cardboard box and a plastic supermarket bag. She put them down on the kitchen floor without a word and looked askance at me.

I studied the box, running my eyes around all the visible edges to determine its dimensions. It seemed to be making scuffling and bumping sounds.

"That box is moving," I said. "What have you got in there?"

"It's an alien creature, rescued from a crashed UFO off the coast of Siberia by a Russian submarine, taken prisoner by the crew and turned over to military intelligence, if that isn't an oxymoron."

I nodded assent. Good grief, 'military intelligence' was almost exactly the best example of an oxymoron that could be found.

"It escaped after three months of questioning, and walked west from Moscow all the way across Northern Europe, sneaking into London by concealing itself in someone's tote bag on the Eurorail. Then it somehow made its way from Waterloo Station to Heathrow airport on the tube before stowing away on a Singapore Airlines flight to Christchurch. I found it raiding a Fendalton organics bin looking for food scraps."

I stared at Chloe in disbelief. She stared back at me without a word.

"Nah," I said eventually. "I do not believe it. There is no way an alien creature could find its way across London on the tube."

Chloe sighed. "I knew I'd gone too far with that one. Okay, it's not an alien creature, it's a little pet for us. A little Aspie pet."

Swiftly, she opened the top of the box. I saw a black and white paw reach out tentatively. A round feline face followed. Then the creature silently hopped out of the box and started to explore its new surroundings.

"A cat? Why is that an Aspie pet?"

"It's a kitten, Robert, and I've heard that all cats have Asperger's Syndrome, so I guess it must be true. Personally, I think they might all be bipolar as well, actually."

"And is he going to live here?"

"She. Our kitten is female. I picked her up from the SPCA. I thought we could all do with a pet in the house, you know, to cheer us up and to celebrate after all the study we've done. It's supposed to be good for the soul, or something."

"I think that is chicken soup. Anyway, what do you mean, 'our kitten'?"

"Well, I thought we would all look after the little thing," said Chloe, shrugging. "Hey, where is she?"

I looked around. There was no sign of the new pet in the kitchen. I went into the living room, looking around. Where would a kitten go? I wondered.

"She is in here, curled up on the sofa," I called out.

Chloe came in. I pointed at the kitten ensconced amongst the sofa cushions, preparing to go to sleep by the look of it. Chloe laid her left arm around my shoulders and leaned her head on my right shoulder. I do not know why she did that, but I did not mind. It felt nice.

"Doesn't she look comfy?" she said, before breaking the spontaneous cuddle and going to sit down on the other sofa, leaving enough room for me. I joined her there. We leaned back into opposite corners. She started twirling the blue hair dangling across her left eye like she often does when she is thoughtful.

"So what is the name of this kitten?" I asked.

"She doesn't have a name yet. We need to give her one. Isn't that cool? We get to name this little creature. Any ideas what we should call her?"

"'Tibbles'?" I ventured. "Or maybe 'Troubles' might be more accurate." I sniggered.

"No," replied Chloe seriously. "It has to be something short and easily remembered, because I'm dyslexic. Otherwise, I'll never manage when I take it to the vet's. Any other ideas? You're the creative one."

Am I? I thought. *Hardly.* "What about 'Tabby'?"

"That's too ordinary. It's got to be something unusual for us, in this house."

"How about 'Tinkerbell'? We would just call her 'Tink' for short."

Chloe lifted her feet up from the floor and swung them into my lap, presumably while she thought about the suitability or otherwise of 'Tink'. She had removed her sandals. I reached out and gently stroked the hard part of the underside of her feet. From the other sofa, the little kitten watched us with one eye open and the other closed, perhaps undecided as to whether to take a quick catnap or listen out to hear us ultimately decide on its name.

"What about 'Sex'?" said Chloe abruptly.

"Sex? You want to have sex?" I said, confused.

"Sure. It's short and easily remembered, so that won't be a problem for my dyslexia. Besides, think about it. Kitten. Sex. Sex. Kitten. They sort of go together, don't they? Like strawberries and cream."

I nodded. *She meant the name of the kitten.* And, in a strange way, it did sound right somehow. "I thought it was peaches that went with cream."

"Whatever. Maybe it's seasonal. Anyway, doesn't she look happy over there? Aw, the little cuddly bundle of fur. I think she's gone to sleep."

Chloe swung her legs back to the floor, got up gracefully and moved over to the other sofa, where she bent over and stroked the kitten gently so as not to wake her up. "Sweet little thing," she said. "There's some kitten food in the bag in the kitchen. Would you mind feeding her when she wakes up, please, Robert? I'm going upstairs to work a bit more on *hatelist.net*."

She went off without waiting for a reply. I sat there for a while, wondering for how long kittens slept on average, and whether or not I could go out and come back before she woke up. I decided against it. Instead, I went upstairs to fetch a book, then returned to the living room, where I curled up on the sofa myself to read, but, like Sex, I was soon fast asleep myself.

Stef loved Sex. Indeed, the little kitten made a tremendous difference to our household. She was always there in the background somewhere, either curled up asleep or playing with kitten toys, providing us with some hilarious entertainment. I could see what Chloe meant about cats having Asperger's Syndrome. Sex was either fearful or curious to extremes, and she needed a lot of 'alone' time. It was impossible to know what she was thinking. She was an absolute mystery to us, yet a delight at the same time. I was truly happy that Chloe had adopted her into our home.

I sat at the kitchen table with my laptop and spent a bit more time using *hatelist.net*, which I found had become addictive, drawing more and more of my leisure time. This time I noticed the title was 'heat slit'. I added the generic term 'investment bankers' to my permanent *hate list*. I had never met an investment banker, but I had recently heard the phrase, 'Give a man a gun, he can rob a bank; give a man a bank, he can rob the world'. That seemed a compelling reason to add them to the *hate list*.

I checked my emails, and came across one that made a chill run through my spine like a cascading snowy mountain stream across bare flesh. It was an email from the FX Trading site with whom I had opened an account (using Chloe's credit card), asking me to revisit their site to do more trading with them.

I sat horrified for a full two minutes. Unconsciously, my right hand withdrew from the mouse, clenched into a fist and started to beat quietly on the tabletop. My breathing deepened. I felt hot, now that the chilling feeling had subsided. I remembered the USD/CHF trade that I had made weeks ago during the time when I was hypomanic.

I had not closed it.

What had I done, exactly? I recalled that it had been an impulsive moment. I had bought US dollars, sold Swiss Francs, for $2 a tick. That meant that a move of even one cent in the exchange rate would cause a profit or loss of $2000 for me, or rather, for Chloe, who did not know anything about it yet. And, of course, in this time the exchange rate may have moved an extreme distance. I may have lost a vast amount of money.

Apprehensively, I logged in to the FX Trading site to check the account. I became aware that I was rocking back and forth in the chair from the nervous tension, chewing the fingernails of my left hand.

Before I could investigate further, Chloe came downstairs and found me. In her hand, she clutched a piece of paper, which ominously looked like some kind of bank statement or, more likely, her credit card statement. I twitched unhappily at this unfortunate serendipity.

I felt nauseated and agitated, and probably looked quite pale, but Chloe (of course) did not notice. That is an Aspie thing. She would rely on me telling her if something was wrong, rather than try to interpret my body language herself.

"Robert, I've got my credit card bill here." She thrust it at me. "You didn't just buy a scooter, did you? There's a menswear shop, food and other stuff too. How much is it, Robert?"

I took the statement from her. Chloe would not trust herself to add up the figures with her dyscalculia, but she would trust me to do it. I quickly identified the expenses that were mine and mentally added them up. I shuddered.

"Four thousand, eight hundred and twenty-seven dollars, seventy-five cents, Chloe. Sorry."

"What's that in single digits?" she demanded, grabbing the statement back from me and pulling a pen out of a pocket somewhere.

"Four—eight—two—seven—dot—seven— five."

She scribbled it down as I said it. I had no idea how I could pay this back. Even if I got another part-time job, it would not pay enough for me to repay this debt for ages, and I usually got fired within a few weeks anyway.

"Look, Robert, I can't pay this either, so I'm going to speak to my father about it. Don't worry—I'll explain what happened, that you—a friend—became ill and used my card number impulsively. He'll probably understand and won't make you pay. He can certainly afford this... What's the matter?"

She had finally noticed my level of despair. Perhaps the fact that I was staring at the carpet between us, instead of thanking her for her kindness, betrayed my inner turmoil in some way.

"It might be a lot more than that," I said. I could not look up at her. Shame seems to increase the effect of gravity on the head and neck muscles in this way. I remained with my head bent down, so she could not see my face.

She sat down on one of the kitchen chairs without speaking. That was unusual for Chloe, and usually signified worry. Perhaps she thought her father might not pay for anything more. Sure enough, in a moment she began running her right hand through her hair, over and over again.

I could be in massive trouble, I realised sadly.

"I started trading FX," I explained unhappily. "Betting on the exchange rate movements. Except that I forgot about it when the depression started. I have got an open trade. I do not know what has happened to it yet. I have only just remembered and was about to check."

"Do it," commanded Chloe briskly, dragging her chair around to sit next to me. She rested her left hand on the back of my chair, as if to hold it in place, so I could not push it back and run off. Not that I intended to do that.

It only took another few seconds to check my position, as I had already logged in. The trade was still live, as I expected. I stared at the green figure on the screen.

"Sixteen thousand, two hundred and forty-eight dollars," I said.

"You've lost over sixteen thousand dollars? Shit, Robert, what are we going to do? I can't expect my father to pay that!"

I turned and looked directly at Chloe for the first time since she had come downstairs. "No," I said shakily and breathed an enormous sigh of relief. "That is the profit. Fortunately, my trade went the right way. Now, just wait there, I am going to close this out."

That took only a few seconds. It is so easy and convenient nowadays to make or lose large sums of money with the click of a button. I closed the trade and withdrew the profit to Chloe's credit card. Then I turned to her.

"All done. That money has gone onto your credit card now, Chloe. That will pay off what I spent, leaving a profit of eleven thousand, four hundred and twenty dollars, twenty-five cents."

Chloe reached up to squeeze my left shoulder with her left hand. "That sounds like a lot. We'll split it, Robert. That'll pay off our course fees for the year. But don't do this again, will you?"

CHAPTER TWELVE

Books read lately:
Way of the Turtle – Curtis Faith (note: this is not a nature book about carapace-carrying creatures; it is a commodities trading strategy book detailing the experiment of the 'turtle traders' who were trained to trade with a system, and subsequently made millions)
Number of sexual encounters:
Sadly, still none

The economic situation has been troubling me for some time. It gives me nightmares.

When World War One broke out, the Reichsbank declared that their banknotes (marks) could no longer be redeemed for gold. The German government needed to finance their war effort, and they were reluctant to raise taxes, so they needed to borrow...and simply bought their borrowings back with brand new money, a process called monetising the debt, which is effectively creating new money. They were able to do that because it was no longer backed by gold...or, in fact, backed by anything except political judgement and public confidence.

Due to rationing, and the weakening of the economy after the war, people did not spend as much as they used to do. Instead, they saved. With a shrinking economy and the falling velocity of money (the speed at which it circulates through the economy), the government printed more banknotes to stave off economic collapse and try to re-inflate the economy. But this did not work as planned, as the worsening economy and rising unemployment induced people to save rather than spend. Prices rose, though, and the government printed more money to try to keep up.

Confidence in the mark fell. The government tried to reduce its depreciation against other currencies by buying marks in the FX markets, but doing so merely led them to spend valuable gold and foreign currency on marks that were rapidly falling in value. By mid-1922, confidence in the currency had all but vanished altogether. Thinking their savings were worthless (which was rapidly becoming the case), the public decided it was better spending them on something—anything—and the hoarded money flooded the economy. Prices rose markedly, insanely, doubling within days, sometimes within hours. Debts and savings were rendered worthless by the rampant hyperinflation. By late 1923, printing presses ran red-hot, night and day, printing new banknotes of ever-increasing denominations. A loaf of bread cost 200 billion marks. People burned bundles of banknotes because it was cheaper than firewood. The economy had collapsed under the sheer weight of money and the rate at which it was being spent.

In 1971, the US government declared that their banknotes (dollars) could no longer be redeemed for gold. That left them able to increase borrowings, and monetise the debt, whenever they desired. The annual public deficit has grown from $30 billion in those days to well over $1 trillion today. An extended period of low interest rates created speculative bubbles in assets such as stocks and property, and high levels of personal debt, while making it less attractive for foreign investors to buy US government bonds. An economic crisis, bringing the worst recession for 70 years, hit in 2008, and a process of deleveraging (debt *reduction) began. This slowed the velocity of money. Wary of falling into deflationary times, and afraid of another Great Depression, a process of quantitative easing (money creation) was started to boost the economy, but much of the newly-created money stayed in banks' coffers as they were too afraid to lend. As it was hoarded, not reaching the real economy at all, there was further money creation... Does hyperinflation beckon?*

In Gold We Trust.

We all loved having Sex in the house. Chloe said we had to keep her inside for the first couple of weeks while she got used to her new home, but even after that she seemed to enjoy nothing more than curling up to sleep on one of the orange sofas, on one of our beds or on one of our laps. From time to time, she would play with one of her kitten toys (Stef called them Sex toys), flicking a little fabric mouse into the air and leaping to catch it between her paws. She was company for each of us when the others were out.

One late Thursday afternoon in June was such a time. It was the mid-year break from university, but Chloe had gone there to re-run some experiments as part of an assignment for her psychology course. She had been annoyed that, although the experiment was the same as when she had done the course last year, her results were different. Stef was at work as usual. I had passed a leisurely afternoon alone apart from having Sex on the kitchen table while I used my laptop for web surfing. Chloe's web app again drew my attention.

I added estate agents to my permanent *hate list* (I do not know why I did that, as I have never bought a house and will probably never be able to afford one, but they do seem to be near the top of everyone's list, so there must be a reason for their unpopularity). The *hatelist.net* title was currently 'this tale'. I looked through Chloe's list for a while too. Nothing much new there. Perhaps she had been spending her time on new features. There was a new part of the website in which you could display an image of an individual on your *hate list* and distort it in various ways, making it a kind of grim caricature or parody of the real person.

After a while, I tired of playing with that and started rocking gently in my chair, mulling over things on my mind, trying to tease out the feelings inside me and understand them. Unlike logic, emotions flow like a dark river, always moving on the surface, and impenetrable beneath. Or so I thought. I knew I was relatively free of worries and concerns. I liked living in this house with Chloe and Stef as flatmates, and I had no debts, having paid off my course fees for the year with my share of the FX trade winnings. Was it a sense of contentment I felt, or happiness? I was not sure, but the change from the depression of a few months previously had been tremendous, like a black-and-white silent movie suddenly bursting into vibrant colour and surround sound.

I evaluated my goals for the year and realised, sadly, that I had made no progress on one of them—that of having sex. I do not mean acquiring a kitten named Sex, but partaking of actual sex itself. With another person. With a woman, that is. Half the year had passed, and I was no closer to finding a girlfriend than at the start of the year. I felt much better about myself, though. At least that was something positive. I truly wanted to find a partner, but I really did not know how to go about it properly.

Sex raised her head to peer at me, perhaps curious or irritated, as my fingers rattled across my laptop keyboard, typing search keywords, googling for internet dating sites in

New Zealand. There were several to choose from, and I picked out one to browse for a while. Perhaps this would be the answer to my dilemma. I checked out the usual pages—Help, FAQ, Terms and Conditions.

As far as I could make out, people wrote profiles about themselves, then looked up the profiles of other people on the site and sent them messages. This was extremely Aspie-friendly due to the lack of body language and physical touch involved. I had a look at several profiles to see what some of the young men had written, and they seemed quite alike—everyone was 'fun-loving', 'cool' and had 'a great sense of humour'. Perhaps only people like that were involved in internet dating, I thought.

I wondered what I would write if I wrote a profile for myself. Maybe something like: 'Young mentally ill Aspie seeks intelligent, attractive woman interested in economics and sex.' It would certainly stand out from the other profiles.

At that moment, the front door crashed open, shaking me out of my introspective thoughts. Stef rushed inside. Even I could perceive she was in some state of excitement. For an apprehensive few moments, I wondered if someone was chasing her, perhaps her ex-boyfriend Jeff, but no one followed her into the house.

I shut down my laptop and waited expectantly to see what would happen next.

"Robert! You won't believe our luck! Look at this email I've got! It's going to make us rich! Filthy rich!" She opened her handbag, pulled out a carefully-folded piece of paper and thrust it at me.

I took it cautiously, as if it was counterfeit money, and I did not want my fingerprints on it, but I took it, nevertheless, simply out of curiosity. I read it through and put it on the kitchen table, shaking my head.

"No, Stef, that is not a good idea."

I was almost sure that she was bursting with excitement still. "No, Robert, you don't understand. I've already had three emails from this guy, and he's the real deal, an investment guru. Of course, at first I thought it was a scam, and I ignored the first three emails, but his predictions all turned out to be true. He tipped a little Australian gold mining company would rocket after mining results—and they did! Then he tipped an African oil explorer would rocket after drilling results—and they did! Then it was a tip that Sterling would fall—and it did! Now this latest email says he's got an even better tip, but I need to subscribe to receive it. It's only a thousand dollars. We could make ten or twenty times that!"

"Stef, it is not what you think—"

"But, Robert, he's been right three times already! Why not a fourth time? It's worth the chance, surely?"

"Sit down, Stef," I sighed.

She sat down and looked across the table at me with an expression I could not decipher.

"Let us say for a moment, Stef, that a thousand people got this email. The one you printed out here." I tapped the paper on the table.

"All the more reason to be quick, before too many people know what the fourth tip is!"

I continued. "What he has probably done is this: initially he sent out eight thousand emails about the Australian gold mining company. In half of them, he predicted the shares would rocket after mining results, as in yours. In the other half, he predicted the shares would crash."

Stef continued to stare at me with an expression I could not fathom. However, she was silent. I took that as a sign to keep explaining.

"He sent the email about the African oil explorer to the four thousand people, including you, who had received the first correct prediction. Remember, four thousand people also got a wrong prediction. It was just luck that you received the correct one. Again, half of the emails predicted the shares would rise, and the other half predicted the shares would fall. Is this making sense to you?"

Stef nodded slowly.

"So now two thousand people, including you, have had two correct predictions, and he makes a third one about the direction of Sterling. And once again you are one of the half who, through random chance alone, receives the correct tip. Now there are a thousand people who have had three correct tips in a row, and they all think the guy is an investment genius. And now," I tapped the printed-out email on the table once more, "he asks those thousand people for one thousand dollars for a fourth tip. Some people will pay up and receive it. But it will simply be luck as to whether it comes out right or not, just like the others."

"I had no idea," said Stef slowly. She picked up the printed-out email, screwed it up and dumped it into the rubbish bin. "Shit, I nearly paid for that subscription before I left work. It was only at the last minute I decided to come home and talk to you about it first."

"It is a devious scam. A con."

"You know, Robert, for someone who doesn't understand people very well, you are actually quite astute sometimes."

"Thanks," I said. I think that was a compliment, but I was not sure.

It was Friday evening. Chloe sat at the kitchen table, working intensively on the facial images distortion feature for *hatelist.net*. I sat in the living room, reading possibly the greatest stock market investment book ever written, *Reminiscences of a Stock Operator*, the fictionalised biography of Jesse Livermore, who made and lost fortunes (several times). *I want to be like him*, I thought.

Stef came home from work and, after putting her bag away, busied herself in the kitchen, as it was her turn to prepare dinner that night, according to our posted schedule. Stef was the only one of us who could actually cook anything worth eating. Chloe and I were often too engrossed in our special interests to leaf through recipe books looking for delicious dinners to prepare, so beans on toast or baked potatoes were usually eaten on our cooking nights.

After a while, I overheard Stef asking Chloe, "Has Sex eaten her dinner yet? I'm just asking because I don't want to give it to her twice."

I sat bolt upright with a strange feeling. Possibly fear, or dread, or anxiety. Uneasily, I looked around the living room, but there was no Sex there. I suddenly realised I had not seen Sex since about lunchtime.

"Chloe!" I called out. "Do you have Sex in the kitchen?"

"No," she called back. "I thought she was with you."

Between us, Chloe and I decided this was an emergency. Stef was all for just waiting, confident that the kitten would turn up later, but I was worried, and so was Chloe. This was not the normal behaviour pattern of our little feline friend.

We looked everywhere we could think of—on and under the beds and chairs, behind the curtains, behind the

TV, outside in the garden. After fifteen minutes, we had searched everywhere in the house and garden that we thought the kitten could possibly be, and we stood together on the porch outside the front door, planning our next move.

Chloe's lips were trembling, and she was showing a hint of lacrimation. I did not know what to do to comfort her. There seemed to be nothing I could do to improve the situation. Sex was nowhere to be found. She had apparently vanished into thin air, like the crew of the Mary Celeste.

Chloe suddenly leaned forward, putting her head onto my right shoulder. Cautiously, I put my left arm around her shoulders. She sobbed twice, then lifted her head and flicked at her dangling blue hair. "Maybe she's run away and got lost. Look, it's dark already. We have to find her before she gets into trouble. Someone might steal her. Someone might already have stolen her! We might never see her again!"

Stef popped her head around the front door. "Dinner's ready," she said. Her facial expression changed. "Haven't you found her?"

"No. She could be anywhere by now," I said.

I did not know what to do. This was not a situation I had been in before, and I could not extrapolate what I should do from any similar event in the past. I did not know whether to eat dinner or go looking for the kitten first. I decided to resolve this by waiting to see what Chloe did, but she also seemed emotionally overloaded. She was twirling her dangling blue hair, making tangled circles with it and then untangling them.

Stef resolved the problem for us. "Quickly, come and eat. Then we'll all go out looking for her. Who knows, she may even come back before we're finished."

We went inside and hastily devoured a tuna and pasta dish topped with grilled crispy ready-salted potato chips, straight from the oven. It was mighty tasty, but all our thoughts (well, mine anyway, and probably Chloe's) were about Sex.

After eating dinner, we went outside and split up. It was dark now. Chloe went left, towards the mall. Stef decided to take the nearest side-streets. I went right, towards the railway track and the industrial parks.

There were a few cars around but not many. Most people would have already made their way home from work. I peered into the grounds of the factories and office buildings that I passed, looking for any sign of shadowy movement, any little flash of white paws or yellow eyes reflecting the starlight or pale moonlight.

I did not know how far Sex might have gone. If she had got lost, perhaps she had continued in the wrong direction, thinking she was on her way home. I vaguely remembered reading stories about cats trekking across half of America, so it did not seem improbable that Sex might have gone several blocks.

I crossed the railway line. There was an abandoned building site ahead of me, an almost barren piece of ground usually used as a car park during the day. I stared at it for ages, straining my eyes for any sign of movement in the darkness. Then, suddenly, there was one.

I darted forward, hoping to catch the kitten before she was hidden again amidst the shadows. "Sex!" I called. "Come here!" But it was too late. She had gone.

I walked slowly and quietly into the building site, taking care not to stumble on the uneven ground. Completed office buildings were on either side, and I veered towards one because it appeared that Sex had run in that direction.

I heard a quiet rustle in the bushes surrounding the office building. I had been right. Now all I had to do was catch her before she got away again.

Suddenly, someone grabbed me by the left arm and swung me around to face him. "What are you doing here, mate?" he said.

The man shone a torch into my lower face, so I could not make out any of his features, but the fact that he had a torch would be immensely helpful. Obviously, Chloe or Stef had asked other people for help. This man had probably come to join me in my search, but I should ask him to make sure.

"I am looking for Sex," I explained. "Are you?"

"What?"

"There, in the bushes. Shine your torch."

The man did as I asked him. My eyes were still dazzled by the torchlight, so I could not see anything of him. I looked at the area of the bushes lit up by the pale torchlight.

The bushes rustled. A plump rabbit hopped out, stared in our direction for a moment, then hopped swiftly into the barren area of land, out of sight.

"It's a bloody rabbit," said the man in a strange voice. "What did you think was going on in there? People having sex? It's a bit cold for that out here, isn't it?"

"No, not people," I clarified. "My little pussy. I have been looking for Sex for over half an hour now."

He shined the torch back at my lower face, which made me blink furiously. I caught a glimpse of some kind of cap on his head, and maybe a uniform, but I could not see him clearly at all. His flashlight was too bright.

"Stop shining that at me," I complained, protecting my

eyes from the glare. Now I could hardly see anything.

"You're coming with me, mate."

Dazzled, I felt him grab me firmly by the forearm and lead me towards the road, where a car waited, its indicators and other lights flashing.

There was another police officer in the car, a woman. She was completing some kind of form or paperwork. The policeman who had found me pushed me into the back of the car before he got into the driver's seat and spoke to his colleague.

"He says he was out looking for sex."

"Oh, is that right?" said the policewoman, turning her head to look at me. "You should try Manchester Street for that. But for now we're going to take you to the Colombo Street police station. There've been reports of prowlers in this area and cars being broken into. We want to question you about that."

"I have not seen any prowlers," I said helpfully.

There was no reply. The car sped off, taking me much farther away from Chloe, Stef and Sex. I pulled my mobile phone out of my jeans pocket and sent a quick text to Chloe to tell her what had happened.

At the police station, I was put into a windowless interview room with nothing but a plastic cup of pale lukewarm coffee for company. I did not intend to drink that, so I waited while it got colder and stimmed by flicking the collar of my shirt rhythmically. I hoped that the others had been more successful with their search than I had been.

Forty-seven minutes passed like that. In that time, I got a text from Chloe, saying she had returned home and found Sex shut in the wardrobe in her room. She had fed her and was just waiting for Stef to get home, so they could come and fetch me in The Frog.

After that time, an older policeman I had not met before, quite portly in build, came into the room, along with a younger man, who stood by the door, otherwise not involving himself in the proceedings. The older man sat down opposite me, fingering his bushy moustache.

"Now," he said, "I want to know why you were prowling around that area of town in the dark, trespassing on private property where you had no right to be. I've been told that you were out looking for sex. Is that right?"

"Yes," I said. Good, Chloe or Stef must have told him all about our lost kitten. "But, as it turns out, it was a waste of time. Chloe had Sex in the wardrobe all afternoon."

"Who's Chloe? Your girlfriend?"

If there was a panic button at the back of my mind, it suddenly got activated at that moment as I realised this policeman and the two who had apprehended me had absolutely no idea of the situation of our lost pet after all.

"Not my girlfriend. My flatmate. My other flatmate is Stef. Please, wait until they get here. They will explain everything."

The policeman decided not to wait. He continued to question me. "Were they having lesbian sex together in the wardrobe?"

I hesitated while a lewd unbidden image uneasily went through my mind. Of course, I could not entirely rule out the possibility. I had not been there. However, it was most highly improbable.

"I meant our kitten. We called our pet kitten 'Sex'. It was a good short name, easy to remember and to spell."

The policeman's eyebrows moved in strange ways. He ground his teeth too. Finally, he said, "Do you expect me to believe that you called your kitten 'Sex'?"

"Yes, I just told you. But it was Chloe who named her, not me."

He ground his teeth again, as if he used to chew tobacco and had continued the mannerism but without the tobacco. I hoped he was not going to spit on the floor. People who chewed tobacco usually did. I had seen that in Westerns on TV.

"Uh-huh. And you were out looking for your kitten, were you? Is that why you were prowling around that area in the dark?"

"I was not prowling. I had seen a movement, but when that other policeman came with his torch, we could see that it was a rabbit. It was hard to see because it was dark. Our kitten, Sex, was lost. You can ask my flatmates. They have found Sex, and now they are coming here."

More strange eyebrow movements. Maybe the policeman stimmed this way, but it was an unusual technique. I recommenced stimming myself by tapping my left foot against the table leg.

"Cut that out," he said.

I stopped it and focussed my attention on a spot on the wall behind him. I did not want to look at him because he was staring at me. That was extremely disconcerting.

"Well, whatever it is you were doing," he said, "it's still trespassing. We've had reports of prowlers and people breaking into cars, and for all I know, you were up to no good."

"I was not having any luck finding Sex," I admitted. I shifted my gaze to a potted plant in the corner.

"Uh-huh. Your kitten, that is. And do you have any proof of this oddly-named kitten?"

"It is written on her collar."

There was a knock at the door, and someone stepped inside. It was the policewoman from the car that had brought me to the police station.

"Sarge, two young women have come in with a kitten. They're at the front desk. I think you'd better have a talk to them."

He heaved himself to his feet and strode out of the room, staring at me all the while. I waited patiently.

Five minutes later, I was released and went home with Chloe and Stef.

Chapter Thirteen

Books/articles read lately:
The Theory of Interstellar Trade – Paul Krugman (a fascinating article examining the question of how interest charges on goods in interstellar transit should be calculated when the speed of travel is close to the speed of light, because the general theory of relativity states that, at such speeds, the time taken in transit will actually be less than the time experienced by a stationary observer, such as the sender or the recipient...)
Number of sexual encounters:
Zero... Beginning to feel hopeless now

I have always known I was different, always felt alone. I never understood why it was that I had so much trouble trying to communicate, or make and keep friends. I thought it was a fault in me, a flaw of some kind. I remember people telling me this from time to time, as if I would only admit this shortcoming, I could somehow just flick an internal switch and become 'normal'. But I could not do that. I wondered whether I was being 'tested' in some way, that if I could just achieve whatever I was supposed to do to blend in, some authority figure would come up to me and tell me that I had 'passed the test', and would be welcomed into society forthwith. But eventually I decided such thoughts of mine were moderately psychotic.

It was an immense relief to receive the diagnosis of

Asperger's Syndrome (ASD). At last, I had a label, a framework for understanding myself, guidebooks and mentors for moving forward in life. It was also saddening in a way, briefly, to realise that this pervasive neurological condition had in part sabotaged so many facets of my life— friends, family, school, (lack of) romantic relationships. But the best thing was discovering that I think, feel and see things in a non-typical way for a reason (because of ASD), and that there are others like me, and it is okay for us to be like this.

It was a Tuesday evening in early July. We were all in the living room. The heat pump dispersed warm air and a soft whirring sound that I found quite soothing. Stef shared one sofa with her new boyfriend, Wayne, on which they were cuddling and sniggering quietly together. They were quite irritating actually; I was trying to read *Freakonomics* on the other sofa, and their incessant whispery chatter and intermittent movement frequently interrupted my reading. Chloe had professed herself tired and was lying down with her head on my lap, turned away from me. Except for stimming by twisting the tassel of a cushion with one hand, she lay still. I used her right shoulder as a book rest. We had Sex, too, on the sofa. She was curled up at the other end by Chloe's feet.

After a while, Stef and Wayne went upstairs without a word to us. I read without distraction until Chloe shifted position, rolling over onto her back, where she stared up at me with her penetrating green gaze and her mouth parted slightly.

I went back to reading. After a few moments, she spoke, but I missed whatever she said because I was intently focussed on my book. She reached up, grabbed it, closed it and dropped it on the floor.

"Robert? You haven't said anything for a long time. What are you thinking? Would you like to do something, like go to a café for a green tea, or go to Borders or somewhere? You know, do something fun together?"

She had asked me too many questions. My mind was whirling with how to answer all of them and yet make it clear which answer belonged to which question.

After a few seconds (the limit of Chloe's patience, normally), she hit me in the chest with the cushion with which she had been playing.

"Are you still not listening to me?" she demanded. "What do I have to do—"

"I am listening," I said hastily. "I had not yet thought of what to say. Um... I do not drink green tea. Borders is closed now. What fun thing were you thinking of?"

"I don't know," she admitted. "I just thought it might be nice to go out somewhere together. You know. Do something fun for once."

"Like go to the library?" I asked.

"Yes, but it's already closed, and if Borders is closed too, I don't know where we could go. There's the cinema, of course, but it's usually too loud, isn't it? We could just have a walk, I suppose."

"It is very cold tonight," I said. "Down to one degree, I think. Perhaps we should stay in. We could have another game of Monopoly."

Chloe shuddered, although it was not cold in the living room because the heat pump was still on. "I'd sooner pull out my own teeth," she said.

That reminded me of something. "I am going back to the dentist tomorrow."

"So soon? You said there was nothing wrong when you

went for your check-up last week. Thursday at three-fifteen. What's happened? Have you got a toothache or something?"

"No, nothing like that. I have not brushed my teeth since my appointment last Thursday."

"Why's that, Robert? What's going on? Have you lost your toothbrush or something? You could have borrowed Stef's. She exchanges body fluids with so many people that one more probably wouldn't make a difference."

"No, I wanted another date with my dentist, Donna."

Chloe stopped twirling the cushion tassel and clenched it tightly. "A dental appointment isn't a date, Robert. Her only interest in you is staring into your mouth looking for plaque and rotting holes and greeblies and other stuff. It's not a social occasion. You're just her client."

"Yes, but I like her. She has a sweet voice and lovely eyes. I cannot see much more of her when she is working on me, of course, because of her mask, but I like her eyes. And eyebrows. They are really manicured or something. Do people manicure eyebrows?"

"No. Do you really think that she'll like you more now that you've got rotting teeth and halitosis?"

"I need some reason for another appointment. I want to ask her out. But that is really difficult when my mouth is propped wide open, and she is prodding around in it with metal implements."

"She'll just tell you to go home and brush your teeth regularly. And floss." She shuddered. "I can't stand flossing, can you? Ooh, it's horrible. And she'll charge you ninety dollars, which, I think, you can't spare. You're not using my credit card number again, are you? You'd better not be."

"I have some money left from my part-time job in the

bakery. I made some dough before I got fired."

Chloe sat up abruptly. I wondered whether she was going to argue with me over this, and if so, why. "She's not AS. You are. She's a professional. You're a student. Hey, she must be years older than you, too. And you don't know anything about her."

"Yes, I do," I retorted. "I stalked her on facebook. I know snippets of information about her from that. I have looked up the electoral register, so I know where she lives. Her phone number is not listed in the phone book, but I have googled her and found it out anyway. And I know other stuff. She is an interesting person."

"That's very Lisbeth Salander," said Chloe, referring to the investigative AS heroine of Stieg Larsson's *Millenium* series, "and it's very impressive, but most NS people would think that was stalking or an invasion of privacy, I expect. Why have you been doing all that? She doesn't know anything about you except the state of your teeth."

I did not like the way Chloe looked at me. Her expression was unusual. Her facial muscles seemed tight. She was still clenching the cushion tassel too. All this made me feel uncomfortable, so I kept silent.

"Sometimes you're a bloody idiot," said Chloe, getting up from the sofa and leaving the room.

I did not know what she meant by that, so I tried to continue reading, but my concentration was gone.

My dental appointment went much the way Chloe said it would. It lasted fourteen minutes, and the conversation was almost entirely one way. Most of the time, I was unable to say anything because my mouth was gaping open while Donna prodded around my teeth looking for creeping decay. She talked to me constantly, though, berating me for not looking after them properly. I felt like a naughty schoolchild, but, unfortunately, there was no detention after the appointment. When it was over, she bade me leave the dental surgery before I had an opportunity to say anything sociable at all.

Ninety dollars for fourteen minutes with Donna was expensive, and I could not afford to do that again. Nevertheless, I resolved to ask her out for a coffee somehow (though she would probably have to buy her own). But how? And when?

I knew from the posts on her facebook page that she went to Zumba on Wednesday evenings. Tonight, in fact. It dawned on me that perhaps, if I went there, I might have the opportunity to talk to her socially. Thanks to my unofficial 'therapist' Chloe's teachings, I was much more accomplished now at starting a conversation and maintaining eye contact. Also, I had been practising looking at Donna's eyes when she was examining my teeth. I felt I should be able to cope with an extended real life eye contact encounter with her now.

I went to Zumba that night. First, I waited discreetly in the shadows some distance from the entrance to the hall to make sure that Donna was coming. After she had gone inside, I followed a couple of minutes later. I felt disorientated and sensorially challenged for a few minutes, as it was crowded in there, with about sixty people moving, jostling, chatting and so on. There was constant sound—feet on the wooden floor, voices talking, the low electronic hum of the music player that had been switched on but was not yet playing music.

Some of the people looked remarkably fit. Others looked decidedly fat, but probably intended to become fit. There were plenty of others between these extremes. Self-consciously, I realised that most of the people there were women. There were no young men at all apart from me. I stood out like a wolf among sheep.

Donna did not notice me, though, or if she did, she did not acknowledge me. Perhaps it was because I was standing a couple of lines behind her. Middle-aged women, surrounding me, moved to the music, some of them with the effortless silent grace of a drake on a lake, while others heaved and grunted like pigs at a crowded trough. I moved jerkily and uneasily, completely unsure of what to do. I decided it might be sensible to follow the movements of the woman directly in front of me. She was probably more than twice my age, yet I struggled to keep up with her. I felt self-conscious with my efforts, which were poor in the extreme, and I felt so uncoordinated that I could barely follow any of the steps at all.

I also felt socially awkward in the class, but only slightly. This was a precisely structured social environment. Everyone knew what they were doing, and they were mostly doing the same kind of thing. My discomfort was simply because it was new to me, and I was terrible at it.

After a while, there was a pause in the music. Some of the people left their space in the lines to drink water from bottles on chairs at the side of the room. A space opened up next to Donna when her Zumba neighbour scuttled off for a drink.

Good, I thought. I swiftly moved up to fill that space.

"Hi, Donna," I gasped, somewhat out of breath.

She turned to face me in surprise. "Robert! Hi. I haven't seen you here before. Are you a Zumba virgin?"

"Yes, I am a virgin all right, and I have never been to Zumba before, either."

Her expression changed and, after a pause, she said, "It'll take you a few sessions before you get into the flow of it."

Concerned that time was running out before the music started up again, I decided to reveal my reason for attending the class without any further delay. "Donna, will you go out on a date with me? For a coffee? Or a green tea?"

"Did you come here just to ask me that, Robert?"

"Yes, I did."

"Well, Robert, I find that a bit creepy, actually."

This confused me. I had not done any creeping at all. I did not know what to say now.

Donna continued. "There'll never be anything between us, Robert."

The music started, and around us people began moving to it in rhythmical fashions. Donna turned away slightly and started dancing to it. I waited half a minute to see if she was going to say anything else, but she did not, so I tried to follow her Zumba dance movements. I felt more self-conscious than before, now that I was in the first line of people, at the front of the class, instead of being in the back line where no one could watch me. I knew that most of the class could see my clumsy virgin Zumba moves. Sweat broke out anew on my forehead as much from nervousness as from exertion. I imagined that most of the class were watching my arrhythmic movements with amusement, although I did not turn around to verify that.

Donna said nothing further and, during another pause in the music, she went to get a drink of water, then returned to stand in a different place in the class, behind and four positions to the side of me. This made me feel more uncertain about what was happening, especially after what she had said to me. Is this part of the dating game, I wondered, the play-hard-to-get bit? Is she a tease? Or had I misheard her because of the cacophony of the class? I certainly did not know. All the possibilities burst into my mind, and I immediately started analysing them, as if trying to put some kind of puzzle together. That was even more exhausting than the exercise.

Finally, the class ended. I breathed a huge exasperated sigh of relief and wiped profuse sweat from my forehead with the front of my shirt. I looked around for Donna, expecting her to be waiting for me, but she was nowhere to be seen.

I rushed outside, hopeful of finding Donna, but, in the darkness, I could not see her at all. As I had earlier seen her arrive at the class by car, I guessed that she would probably be walking to where she had parked in the car park. I hurried in that direction.

After a few moments, I caught sight of her and called out to her to wait for me, but it seemed that she did not hear. I quickened my pace and rapidly caught up to her.

She spun around to face me as I approached. "Robert! Are you following me? What do you want?"

"A date," I said, quite out of breath. "Remember, I asked you in the class. You said, 'there will never be anything between us'. I am so happy you feel that way about me and want to be my girlfriend. Shall we go out for a coffee or green tea?"

"Are you crazy? I don't want to be your girlfriend. Are you following me?" she repeated. I noticed that her voice had risen an octave.

"Yes. So I could talk to you."

"Stop following me. I don't want to go out with you."

I was silent for a few moments, dumbstruck. Again I wondered if this was part of the dating game, but I did not think that was likely. Something seemed wrong, but I honestly did not know what it was.

"I do not understand," I said hesitantly. "You told me that nothing could keep us apart."

"I told you that there'll never be anything between us," she snapped at me, which confused me even more, as that seemed to mean the same thing.

"Just keep away from me. You're scaring me," she said, trembling in the chilly evening air.

I had not meant to frighten her. Actually, I was afraid myself. The world is a scary place when you do not understand what is going on, when you are encircled by an impenetrable social fog, when you do not know how to cope in social situations.

Donna backed away a few steps, then turned and walked briskly to her car, looking back at me over her shoulder every few steps. I stood there in the dark, watching her open the door of a sleek red BMW, slip inside, shut the door, start the car and drive off past me. I listened to the sound of her car engine fade in the distance. Other people were coming out of the Zumba class into the car park now.

CHAPTER FOURTEEN

Books read lately:
Market Wizards – Jack D Schwager (note: this is not some kind of fantasy book in which entrepreneurial sorcerers sell their spells; it is a collection of interviews with top stock market traders...)
Number of sexual encounters:
Frustratingly still zero

I am a recent convert to facebook. At first I doubted its usefulness for me, for I had only four facebook friends, and one of those was my mother, who only uses her account to check up on me. But I soon came across a vast global network of Aspies online. And online friendships are superb for Aspies, whether these are with other Aspies or with NS people. It is ideal being able to chat with friends without actually having to spend time with them or even ever be in their presence. I can make virtual friends, get to know them in absolute safety, and, if I find them tedious or objectionable, I can remove them forever with the click of a button. If only it was possible to eliminate family and acquaintances in the real world so easily. I can exchange thoughts with similar-minded people to me in France, England, the United States and other places whom I will never actually meet in person. It is as if the facebook system was designed for Aspies specifically, rather than the entire population, 99% of which are NS.

What I do not understand particularly well is why it is so popular in the NS world. I had always thought that NS people like to interact in person, rather than through a computer. I have read that 70% of personal communication is non-verbal, which we Aspies have trouble with, but, through the computer, this component of communication is reduced to a minimum. Through facebook, NS people cannot convey their coded meanings through contorted facial expressions, body posture and limb movement, or fluctuating tone of voice. In effect, through facebook they must interact on the same level as Aspies—through literal words alone. At last, Aspies are no longer so disadvantaged in the realm of social networking now that it has gone online.

Eight days passed, and I was still thinking about what had happened (or, rather, what had not happened) with Donna, but there was no point in punishing myself further. Stef sat me down and told me off for stalking Donna, wagging her finger at me as if I was a naughty schoolboy who had been caught pinching sweeties. She told me that I would have to change dentists and, sure enough, two days later, a letter arrived from the dental surgery confirming that I would no longer be able to gaze ponderously into Donna's beautiful blue eyes while she explored my teeth with a periodontal probe.

Chloe had not talked to me much since I had gone for my date at the dental surgery. I knew she had been making more enhancements to *hatelist.net* though, so, being curious, I fetched my laptop, sat at the kitchen table and logged in. I noticed immediately that the title had changed to 'hate silt', yet another dyslexic anagram, and that Chloe had added 'dentists', and Donna specifically, to the bottom of her permanent *hate list*. I had to scroll down three screens to find them. I considered for a moment or two before copying them to my own list. I decided I would sooner let my teeth rot than return to see Donna again, which was ironic really, because just two weeks before I had decided to let them decay so I had a reason to see her.

It was my turn to prepare dinner that day, and I made ciabatta sandwiches with brie, apple and ham filling (because it was a Wednesday), my only exception to the beans on toast or baked potatoes fare that I usually prepared. Somehow these distinctive and varied flavours and textures combine perfectly, but it is a combination I have only ever seen in one café.

"Um, guys, I need to tell you something," said Stef as we were finishing off our delicious sandwiches. "My friend Marianne is away this weekend, so she can't have the party at her place, and...well...some of us decided that someone should hold a party anyway, and then we had a kind of a vote...and..."

"No! You're not going to say that you lost the vote, and the party will be here, are you?" demanded Chloe.

"No, I won the vote, and the party will be here. I realise that might not suit you guys, but it's just one night, and probably not many people will come to it because it won't be all of Marianne's crowd of friends, just a few."

"Well, I planned to do my Econ one-oh-one assignment on Saturday night," protested Chloe. "What about you, Robert?"

"Yes, I—"

"And then work more on my web app until the early hours. How can I do that if there's music blaring throughout the house? I assume there'll be bloody loud music. I'm not going out. Why should I? Anyway, there's nowhere to go on a Saturday night. I'm not happy about this, Stef."

"Sorry, Chloe. It's just one night, remember, and it's up to you whether you stay or go out or join the party."

"It's just like the Uni halls of residence all over again," grumbled Chloe.

"I think the parties there were smaller and quieter than those at Marianne's house," I said, trying to clarify the matter.

"Whatever. I'm going to do my assignment anyway. It's on my plan for Saturday."

"I'm going to announce the party on facebook today," said Stef, "so everyone knows where to come."

On Saturday night, I started work on my assignment immediately after an early dinner. It did not take me long. By 8.14 p.m., I had finished it. I wondered whether to offer to help Chloe with hers but decided against it. She would probably ask me if she wanted assistance. She had Sex in her room. We both thought the level of noise from the party would be too much for our little kitten to let her go downstairs.

The party had already started, but the music was not as loud as I had expected. Perhaps Stef had remembered how sensitive we both are to loud noises and was keeping the volume down to avoid assaulting our sensibilities. There was a buzz of voices also. The music and talking were disturbing us, making us feel on edge.

I started to read *The Alchemy of Finance* while sitting on my bed. I felt a little irritated that I could not go down to the living room to read, but that would be impossible with a party going on. I felt as if my space had been invaded, that my comfortable room, normally such a quiet refuge, had temporarily become a prison for me.

I had got through only a single chapter when I became

aware that the music had suddenly been turned up a lot. It was now blaring so much that the floor itself was vibrating to the beat. Yet even this rumbustious musical cacophony did not drown out the sounds of people, which had also become much, much louder. I could hear voices shouting in the front garden and downstairs. There was also the sound of shattering glass outside. I looked out of the window and gasped. The front garden was full of people swigging from bottles (I guess this was because we did not have enough glasses for everyone). One man unloaded a crate of bottles from the back of a white van parked illegally across our driveway. There were cars parked in the street for as far as I could see in both directions (twenty-two of them), and people were arriving in small groups, congregating outside on the footpath and the edge of the road.

I heard a muffled thumping at my door. This startled me, and I dropped my book onto the floor by the window. Chloe entered, cradling Sex in one arm and her laptop in the other. The music boomed even more with the door opened, but she quickly slammed it closed to muffle the noise a little. She said something to me, but I did not hear what it was.

"What did you say?" I shouted across the room. She strode towards me, put her laptop on the floor, thrust Sex into my arms and wrapped her own around me in a tight embrace. I was frightened that our little kitten would be squashed or smothered, but Chloe quickly drew away.

Her eyes were moist with lacrimation. She leaned forward and spoke loudly into my right ear with a timbre in her voice that I had not heard before. "They're on the stairs, they're coming upstairs! What shall we do? I don't want to be alone in my room anymore. I mean, just Sex and me. I hate all these people!"

"Perhaps we should go out after all. We could take our

laptops to McDonald's and work there." I could barely distinguish my own words from the background clamour, and I knew what I was saying. I did not know if Chloe heard or understood me.

Sex was making an odd sound, quite unlike her normal meow, but something like a cross between that and the shriek she made when I accidentally stood on her paw last Thursday morning. I noticed that Chloe was panting. She was clearly becoming overloaded. I shoved Sex back into her arms, so she could stim by stroking the kitten and, perhaps, calm herself and Sex at the same time.

I turned towards the door, opened it and stepped outside into the landing. Chloe was right. There were eleven people standing on the stairs, drinking, smoking, hugging, laughing. I did not recognise any of them from Marianne's parties. I saw the contents of glasses being spilled onto the stair carpet, a cigarette being extinguished against the wall and the butt dropped to the floor, men and women groping each other awkwardly.

The music, if anything, had been turned up another notch. Instinctively, I put my hands over my ears to try to block out some of it, but to little avail. I watched a young woman stagger towards the toilet at the other end of the hall and drop onto her knees.

The door to Chloe's room was open. I reached out to close it and saw six people inside her room, sitting on her bed or standing, drinking and smoking. I called out to them, "Hey, you cannot stay in there! That is my flatmate's room! Please leave!"

The man nearest the door must have heard me. He turned and glared in my direction. He had a clean-shaven head, a tattoo on the side of his face and looked in his mid-thirties. I did not recognise him. He stepped towards me aggressively. Instinctively, I took a step back. He snarled something at me which I did not hear (though I imagine it was unpleasant in tone and content) and slammed the door.

I waited a few moments, trying to think of what to do. I did not think I could make them leave Chloe's room, but I knew Chloe would want her red beret, as she always wears that when she is stressed. I opened the door to her room as quickly and quietly as I could, stepped across to the chest of drawers and opened the drawer in which I knew she kept it. I grabbed it and left the room, holding my breath. The whole move took me only five seconds, and if anyone noticed me, he or she did not care about what I was doing.

I stepped back into my own room and shut the door. Chloe was sitting on the edge of the bed, still cradling and stroking Sex. She rocked back and forth in an exaggerated motion, shaking her head. I hurried over to her and gave her the red beret. She put it on and smiled at me briefly.

"We cannot go down the stairs!" I shouted. "Too many people!"

Chloe stood, handed Sex to me and went over to the window. I wondered if she was thinking of escaping by shimmying down the drainpipe or something, but I knew I could not do that if I had Sex at the same time.

Holding Sex, who was still meowing strangely, with my left arm, I grabbed the chair from my desk and leaned it against the door, propped up under the door handle like I had seen done in crime programmes on TV. Unfortunately, there was no key to lock the door. The chair would have to do.

Chloe sat down on the bed again, and I joined her there. She leaned against me with her head on my left shoulder. I now had an ear-splitting headache and was nearing the point of overload myself, but still coping somehow. Chloe put her right arm around my shoulder for support. We sat together, still and quiet, tensed and anxious, unsure what to do, while all around us in the house and garden continued the most tremendous din.

Nearly a minute later, Chloe gasped and pointed at the door. I looked and saw the door handle rotating and the door rattling as if it were being shaken from outside. For a few seconds, the chair held it closed, but I could see its back legs slipping. It was going to give way any moment. Chloe said something which I did not catch, got to her feet and tugged me to get me to do the same. She grabbed her laptop and mine and scrambled underneath the bed with them. I followed, carefully cuddling Sex. There was not much room, but there was enough to conceal us both. We lay prone there, shoulders touching gently, faces towards each other, one arm each over our laptops. Sex, possibly sensing some kind of refuge here, snuggled in between us and curled up quietly.

I heard the blast of music increasing as the door was forced open. From underneath the bed, I watched the chair scraping across the floor as the door swept it aside. Two people came in, and the door was closed again. Oddly, the chair was put back as it had been, propped up under the door handle. I heard faint sounds of laughter over the blare of the music.

I could only see the lower part of their legs, but their footwear showed that the couple was a man and a woman (unless one of them was cross-dressing, of course). They came closer and closer, then collapsed together onto the bed above us. Seconds later, their footwear fell to the floor, one shoe at a time.

For a short while, we saw nothing and heard nothing except the din of the party in the rest of the house and outside, but then a pair of jeans fell onto the floor not far from where our heads were. Another pair followed, and a blouse, a shirt and other small items dropped in succession to the floor around the periphery of the bed.

Chloe lay next to me holding her breath, her eyes wide open. I reached out and pressed my hand against hers, rhythmically applying and releasing pressure. It was a kind of mutual stimming that felt very pleasant. Chloe smiled at me slightly and started breathing normally. My own level of tension eased fractionally.

Between us, warmed by our bodies, Sex appeared to have gone to sleep. From above us, there came a new sound—a periodic creaking of the springs of the old bed.

Abruptly, the music downstairs was turned off or down to a volume at which I could not discern it. There was a lot of shouting from everywhere—the stairway, downstairs and outside. I could hear car doors slamming. All this made little difference to the activity of the couple on the bed above us. The creaking of the springs had discernibly increased in amplitude and frequency.

Once again the door began to shake as someone tried to open it and, as before, the chair held it closed for a few seconds before it burst open. Someone came in and called out, "Police! Everyone out of the building! Phoaar! And cover yourselves up decently first."

It was a voice I recognised. It was the policewoman who had driven me to the police station a few days earlier when I had been out looking for Sex.

By unspoken mutual agreement, Chloe and I lay still and quiet. Two pairs of naked feet and legs landed on the floor next to the bed. Hands reached down to pick up the discarded items of clothing. The shoes were bumped upright, and feet thrust into them.

Stef appeared in the doorway. Unless it was someone

else with similar legs and shoes. But that doubt was removed after the policewoman asked her, "Do you know these two?" and she replied, "No, I've never seen either of them before."

"Right, downstairs, Romeo and Juliet," said the policewoman. "Give your names and addresses to the constable at the door."

The couple walked quietly to the door, and Stef let them get past on their way to the stairs. I wondered how the policewoman knew their names, and how ironic it was that they shared the names of the lovers in Shakespeare's play.

At that point, Sex woke and sprang out from under the bed into the centre of the room, where she paused to lick her feet. I sighed. *Surely, now we would be discovered. Would that lead to more awkward questions?*

"Sex!" cried out Stef.

"Yes, that's right," said the policewoman. "It seems that people will do anything when they gatecrash a party."

"No, no, I mean our kitten. I was so worried about her." Stef strode over quickly and bent down to cuddle our little pet. She caught sight of Chloe and I under the bed and smiled. "And you two, too."

"It's all right," said Chloe as we crawled out, "we had Sex under the bed to keep her safe."

"You two again!" exclaimed the policewoman, frowning and making a face. Was that a wry smile, a smirk, a look of disgust or something else she made? I did not know.

"We live here," I said, as if that explained everything. It justified why Sex was here, anyway.

"Who had sex under the bed?" came a gruff voice I also recognised, and the portly figure of the sergeant hove into view. He saw me. His eyebrows started moving strangely, and he ground his teeth like he was chewing tobacco. I hoped he was not going to spit on the floor in my room.

"You two and your kitten with the stupid name again?" he finally growled.

"It's not stupid," retorted Chloe. "You remembered it, didn't you? How often do you remember strangers' pets' names?"

He scowled and turned away. I heard him stomping down the stairs.

Stef, still holding Sex in her arms, embraced Chloe and me briefly. "I'm sorry, really sorry. It started out fine, just like an ordinary party at Marianne's, and then heaps of strangers turned up and gatecrashed. They took over the house. You won't believe what a mess it is downstairs."

"Why not?" I asked. *Why would it be unbelievable?*

The policewoman spoke up. "This isn't the first time this sort of thing has happened, you know. There're groups of troublemakers who look out for these things, parties announced publicly on facebook instead of confined to a group of friends. Inevitably, the police have to get involved to restore order."

"I'm so sorry," repeated Stef. She burst into tears. Helpfully, I reached out and took Sex from her arms in case she started crying uncontrollably. I saw that Chloe was busy fetching our laptops from under the bed.

CHAPTER FIFTEEN

Books read lately:
Anatomy of the Bear: Lessons from Wall Street's Four Great Bottoms – Russell Napier (note: this is not a text about the physiology of bears or a biography of four overweight 'fat cats' of the business world; it is about historical stock market declines, so-called 'bear' markets...)
Number of sexual encounters:
Still not even one

I do not 'get' other people, and they do not 'get' me.
   "People who understand the things I don't understand, can't understand how anyone cannot understand them." – a child with Asperger's Syndrome.

The second semester at Uni continued with Chloe and I sticking to our practice of meeting in the café on Mondays, Tuesdays (twice), Thursdays and Fridays. It seemed natural to continue doing this even though we had been flatting together for months, ate meals together most days and studied an average of 6.4 hours a week together. In fact, I do not think either of us had ever suggested that we break the pattern of spending our free time at Uni together.

However, one afternoon in late August, something unexpected happened to change this. I arrived seven minutes early at the café and quickly settled myself at the usual corner table with a cappuccino to read *The Battle For Investment Survival*.

I was so absorbed in this fascinating book that I did not notice Chloe arrive in the café until she approached the table, drink in hand. She wore tight blue jeans and a green sleeveless top (as it was a Thursday). She eased into the seat next to me, adroitly setting her handbag and cup of green tea on the table. But what startled me was that someone else pulled out the chair next to her and sat down too.

Frowning, I regarded him suspiciously while he settled himself, ripped open three paper tubes of raw sugar and poured all of them into his mochaccino at the same time. *Why did he have to intrude on the time Chloe and I spend together?* I wondered. *We have shared this time between ourselves five times a week for months. It just does not seem right that someone else sits here too. There are plenty of other tables available.*

I watched as Chloe turned to face him, smiled and reached out to pat his arm with her left hand. "This is my flatmate, Robert," she said, gesturing towards me with her other hand.

I did not say anything. It was now evident that she had invited him to join us, or at least knew who he was and did not mind him invading our table.

"Hi, Robbie," said the interloper with a thick accent that I did not recognise. He did not look directly at me. Perhaps because I was scrutinising him so intently.

He was another student. I did not know him, but I had seen him around the campus, so he was a familiar stranger. He had dark brown eyes and a wide lopsided grin. He wore a dark brown hoodie (with the hood down) and blue jeans. His ears seemed uncommonly large, virtually elfin in appearance, and the mass of black hair on his head was thick and tousled. He had a little dab of a beard above his chin, so small it looked like a ridiculous shaving mistake.

"My name is Robert," I said.

"Sure, Robbie," he grunted, glancing across at Chloe and tapping the table in front of her with a podgy index finger.

"Oh, Robert," said Chloe, turning to me. She was not smiling now. "I've been having some fascinating conversations with Cliff. He's from my Sociology class. He's a self-diagnosed Aspie, and he's started up a new university special interest group—"

"BAND," interrupted Cliff, looking at me for the first time. His eyes were hard and intense. I immediately looked away, observing the checkout queue absent-mindedly while he prattled on. "BAND stands for 'Ban Autism Neurodiversity Discrimination'. I, or rather we, once there's more of us, want to make it socially unacceptable, even illegal, to discriminate against people with ASD in the workplace."

"Because otherwise we'll struggle to get jobs after Uni," added Chloe, pulling a pen from her handbag. She started to spin it horizontally in her right hand, one of her ways of stimming that I find mesmerizing, and particularly because she could do it in either hand. "The corporate world only wants people who conform, who follow the leaders, who are team players. It doesn't want people who think for themselves, are creative and individualistic. So that rules us out of most of the high-paying jobs."

"Uh-huh." *That rules us out of most of the low-paying jobs too*, I thought.

"It's a war," continued Cliff, now staring intently at me while I watched the queue at the checkout move slowly along. "Us against them. The establishment, I mean. And the proletariat, the mob. The corporate world, the health system, the education system. Hollywood. Bollywood. They're all against us in one way or another. But we're going to get organised and fight back. We're going to protest. Just like the gays did. They support us, you know. Do you get where I'm coming from?"

"I have no idea where you came from," I said slowly and gulped down the rest of my cappuccino. Chloe and Cliff seemed to have forgotten their drinks, for they had not touched them since they had sat down.

Chloe reached out and stroked Cliff's arm before turning back to face me, this time with a smile. "Cliff has such grand plans for the Aspie community. Did I tell you he diagnosed himself with Asperger's? He's going to change everything. He'll bring us—"

"I'll bring us to the forefront of public thinking. I'll get in their face. Faces, I mean. I—I mean we—will change public opinion of Aspies and Auties. We'll show them that we're not just geeky freaks and obsessive nerds without any social skills. We're much more than that. We just need to get our message out there."

"What is the message?" I asked, looking directly at Cliff. I noticed that Chloe beamed a wide smile at him again. She was still stroking his arm, but he did not seem to notice it.

"Some of the greatest thinkers of all time probably had undiagnosed ASD," said Cliff, looking away and focussing intently on a spot on the grubby café floor by our table where there was a coffee spill from last Monday. "Einstein, Mozart, Tesla, Sherlock Holmes. Imagine if they had been shut out of life because they weren't 'team players'. That's the message."

"How is that going to help us get high-paying jobs?" I asked. I did not like Cliff, and I did not know why I felt that way, but I thought some of what he had to say was mildly intriguing. Though most of it was bollocks.

"It's all about educating people," said Chloe. "Make them aware—"

"We've got to garner public support and gain acceptance," interrupted Cliff again. He did not seem to notice when Chloe was talking, or perhaps he was already familiar with her version of verbal diarrhoea and wanted to cut her short before she got into her stride and became unstoppable. "We'll have rallies and protest marches. We'll storm parliament, if we can get a social welfare grant to pay our airfares to Wellington. And we'll write letters." He nodded and grinned widely as if this simple plan would be the solution to our community's woes.

"It'll be great!" said Chloe, her sea-green eyes sparkling. "People will see and hear our message. Cliff will get it out there. People will listen. They won't ignore us any longer. They'll see we can make a contribution. It just needs education and understanding—"

"And if they don't listen, we'll rise up and take over the government," said Cliff, gazing in my direction again.

I looked away to check how the checkout queue had changed. Seven people waited to pay. Cliff continued talking, but I did not listen closely anymore. I was bored with his ramblings and wished he would depart and leave Chloe and me in peace.

"Or we might start our own nation state," continued Cliff. "Like Israel, but better, because it won't be in the desert. We'll petition the government for our own land and right to rule ourselves. Maybe they could give us South New Brighton or that waste ground in Bexley near the sewage works for us all to settle in. Once there's enough of us in BAND to start a new elite society, of course. I'll be the first President."

Chloe looked at him with wide-open eyes and a happy smile on her face. She still had not let go of his arm, yet Cliff appeared unaware of her attentions as he tried to convince me of the merits of his banal (and perhaps mildly insane) ideas.

"Is it not the case that presidents should be elected?" I asked pointedly, shifting my attention to the inside of my empty coffee mug.

"I meant a benign dictatorship at first. We'll transition to elective democracy in due course."

"How many members have you got in BAND?" This was out of politeness, for I actually did not give a shit.

"It's just started," said Cliff evasively. "I'm sure membership will grow quickly once word gets around. We're going to meet once a fortnight in a secret location to plan our strategies."

I had to ask. "If your meetings are in a secret location, how will people know where to go?"

"It's not a problem at present. I haven't arranged the first meeting yet. Are you interested in joining, Robbie?"

"No," I said. "And my name is Robert."

Chloe grinned widely and fondled his arm with her slender fingers. Cliff reached over and patted her hand. I did not like that. He should ask before touching someone in case they are touch-sensitive or OCD about germs and such. But Chloe did not seem to mind. If anything, she smiled even more. I ground my teeth and started stimming by tapping my left foot against the metal chair leg so it made a satisfying clunking sound. I wondered if I could think of something to say to make Cliff go away.

"Cliff, go away," I said.

"Oh, don't be like that, Robert," said Chloe, pulling a face at me, but I did not know if she was upset at what I had said or if she was trying to be funny.

Cliff did not move. Even worse, he resumed talking. "We must all band together, Robbie. Band together, get it? Like the acronym 'BAND'. Together we stand tall, divided we fall through the cracks of society."

"Yes, I get it," I said wearily. "Very idealistic."

"Isn't he a genius?" said Chloe. "And his plans are so cool."

"Positively chilling," I said.

After a while, Cliff actually did leave but, unfortunately, Chloe went with him, so she and I did not have our usual break and chat together. I missed that. I actually felt lousy about it, as if I had gone to the cinema to see a new film and the screening had been cancelled because the projectionist and ticket seller had run off together to Bognor Regis or Kaiapoi and the place was empty. But it was me that felt empty. I always enjoyed my chats with Chloe in the café. I guess that is why I felt a little frustrated.

Also, we normally talked for twenty-seven minutes in the café on Thursdays, giving us both just enough time to get to the next lecture, but not today, for Chloe had departed with Cliff eight minutes sooner. I had unstructured time that I suddenly had to fill, and I decided to walk to the bookshop to browse the science fiction and economics shelves.

I had gone only seventeen paces from the café when someone fell in beside me. Another student, probably. I had seen him around the campus, but I did not know anything about him. He was roundish in shape and wore spectacles, loose jeans and a nondescript sweater. His chubby cheeks were red, and he had a wide smile. His brown hair looked a little bit out of control.

"I saw you talking to that guy Cliff," he said in a low voice. "You should watch out for him. There's something very strange about him. You should warn your girlfriend about him, you know."

I stopped walking and turned to face him. "Chloe is not my girlfriend. She is my flatmate."

"That's even more reason to be wary of him. Trust me, he's all talk, and it's mostly sweet talk."

"He did talk a lot, but he never mentioned confectionery. Who are you?"

"You can call me James."

He stuck out his hand. I was probably meant to shake it but out of general principles I did not. I do not like touching strangers because I do not know what their personal hygiene habits are like. James looked clean, but you could never be too sure.

"What do you know about Cliff?" I asked James as he withdrew his hand. He kept smiling broadly at me. He seemed to be a genuinely friendly guy.

"He's up to something," whispered James. "I've been following him for a few days. He's started some kind of organisation. Probably a subversive one. I don't know what it is, but I'm watching him, and I'm going to find out."

"Why are you so interested in him?"

"Look, I shouldn't tell you this, you know, but I'm part of the Student Intelligence Service."

"I have never heard of them," I said.

"Of course you haven't. We're very secretive. No one has heard of us. We're even more secret than the West Melton Crashed Aliens Dissection Laboratory or the Merivale Illuminati Preschool."

"I have never heard of them either," I said.

"Never mind. The point is, I know that Cliff is up to something. I want to know exactly what. That's my mission."

"Why are you telling me this?"

James leaned in closer to me and lowered his voice even more. I think it may have been because he did not want anyone else to hear what he was about to say. However, his whispering had the effect of making me much more interested in listening.

"I need your help. Your flatmate is close to him. You can ask her what his organisation is all about. Find out their movements. What their plans are."

"He did say something about storming parliament," I said. "Is that helpful?"

"Certainly," said James, whipping a small notebook and a pen out of his jeans back pocket and quickly writing an illegible note. "Anything else of importance?"

I considered, playing back in my mind all of what Cliff had told me. I did not like doing this, because it replayed in the sound of his voice, which I found intensely irritating.

"Not really," I said.

"If you think of anything, let me know. Here's my number." James pulled a white card that was the size of a normal business card out of another pocket and pressed it into my hand. I saw there was nothing but a hand-scrawled cellphone number on it.

I did not actually want to talk to him any longer. I was

now late for my next lecture, and I would have to sneak in through the side entrance. That did not bother me, but it would be inconvenient. "I have to get going now," I said.

James grinned even wider, showing gleaming white teeth. He reached out and patted me on the shoulder with a chubby hand. I restrained myself from hitting back at him for this unwelcome physical contact. Instead, I turned away from him.

"I'll be talking to you again," I heard him say as I briskly walked off.

I fretted more than usual that day. I think it was moodiness that I felt. I barely spoke to anyone, and sometimes I bumped into other students as I ventured across the campus because I was too preoccupied with my thoughts about Chloe's uncharacteristic behaviour to watch where I was walking. She had shown far too much interest in Cliff, hanging onto his arm and listening to him blethering away about his ambitious and ridiculous plans. She did not even drink any of her green tea.

I also found myself dwelling on what James had said regarding Cliff, which was not much altogether, and only about thirty-five percent of it had made any sense to me at all. It was sixty-five percent mysterious. I could not help but try to fill in the gaps of my knowledge of Cliff with my own assumptions and suppositions about him and the aims of his odd organisation. These thoughts of mine tended to be negative. I became more and more worried about Chloe and what she might get into if she continued to associate with him. *No doubt about it, Cliff is a strange guy, all right. Though James might be trustworthy, his background seems rather murky, too.* I tend to trust people immediately, but for some reason I did not understand, I had an uneasy feeling about Cliff, and that made it all the easier to believe

James's condemnations of him.

I pondered them both all day. My mood had slightly improved when I got home from Uni late that afternoon, but I quickly regained my composure when I encountered Stef in the kitchen cooking our dinner. A giant frying pan of Bolognese sauce simmered on the front of the hob, and a steaming pot of boiling spaghetti sat at the back.

Stef turned to me with a smile and said 'hello'. There were spatters of sauce on her plastic apron, but she did not seem to mind them, or perhaps had not noticed how the red splotches randomly blemished its sunflower patterning. I resisted the urge to wipe them off with a paper towel because she might consider that constituted inappropriate physical contact. Then I noticed that there were four dinner plates laid out on the bench top instead of three, and I promptly forgot about the splattered sauce.

"One of Chloe's friends is staying for dinner," said Stef as I pointed at the fourth plate with a querulous finger. "She said you know him too. A guy called Cliff."

I groaned.

"What's he like, Robert?" whispered Stef. She glanced at me quickly before turning her attention back to stirring the sauce with a wooden spoon. "I think Chloe fancies him."

"Does she? I had not noticed." I paused, contemplating what I could say about Cliff that might not be libellous or inflammatory. There was not much to choose from. "Cliff talks a lot," I offered.

"I'd be amazed if he could out-talk Chloe." Stef grinned at me.

"Prepare to be amazed," I said, and then went to set the table for dinner.

Chloe and Cliff sat together on one of the orange sofas,

talking. More precisely, Cliff was expounding on one of his outlandish theories with sweeping hand gestures, and Chloe sat still, staring at him in wonderment. They ignored me, and I ignored them, as I lay the place mats and cutlery in a symmetrical pattern on the dining table. I noticed a large, scruffy backpack leaning against the wall in the corner of the room. It was packed full and loosely done up. There was no sign of Sex. Perhaps she had the sense to find somewhere quieter to rest. Probably on my bed, I thought.

As I expected, Cliff continued to talk virtually all the way through dinner, stopping only momentarily to messily bolt down a forkful of Stef's favourite dish, 'spag bog'. He barely glanced at the food and would not look directly at either Stef or I, but he quite studiously appraised the features and furnishings in the room. Idly, I wondered if Chloe planned to give him the same 'eye contact' lessons she had taught me.

The first ideas he presented to us (with the blustery showmanship of a circus ringmaster) at dinner were not too bizarre. There was no talk of storming parliament or creating a separate nation state this time. He talked again about equal opportunities in the workplace, a subject that was pertinent to most of us, as none of us, except Stef, who is NS, had been able to hold down even a casual part-time job for long. But, after a while, the conversation (or should I say lecture) abruptly changed direction.

"No one really knows the causes of autism, except of course we know there is a strong genetic component," declared Cliff. Chloe nodded vigorously. I said nothing, but continued to listen. I already knew this.

"The incidence of autism is not rising," went on Cliff, "but it is more widely recognised and diagnosed nowadays than in even the recent past. Unfortunately, the media sometimes portrays a diagnosis of ASD in a child as a tragedy."

"Utterly fucking ridiculous," said Chloe vehemently.

Cliff barely glanced in her direction before continuing. "We must change this negative public perception. We are not freaks, merely deviants. ASD is a difference, not a disorder. Yet some would-be parents are demanding pre-natal tests for autism."

"That's not possible, is it?" asked Stef. "There's no such test yet."

"And there should never be," declared Cliff. I was listening intently by now, for he was actually making sense with this, so far.

"Why?" asked Stef, who had not worked it out yet. "Wouldn't that be scientific progress?"

"Of course it is," snapped Chloe. "But that isn't the point, Stef. Not all progress is positive. It might give would-be parents the choice they think they want, but that isn't good."

"There's a pre-natal test for Down's Syndrome," said Cliff. "What happens to most of the foetuses diagnosed with that?"

"Um... They get aborted?" guessed Stef quietly.

"Over ninety percent of them," said Cliff. "Including, of course, the ones that were wrongly diagnosed in the womb by the test. If a pre-natal test for autism is ever developed, the same thing might happen. Only about one in a hundred people have ASD. With a test like this, it might fall to one in a thousand."

"And our community would be decimated nine times over," I chipped in. I agreed with Cliff on this grave matter. It was a relief to me that not all of his views and opinions were nuts. This one was quite serious.

Stef nodded grimly. Now she understood, I thought.

"Shit, I probably wouldn't be here if that test existed," said Chloe.

"I have a plan," declared Cliff, looking around us without making eye contact. "BAND will oppose any research into pre-natal testing for autism, naturally. But that will only serve to keep our numbers stable. We will still be far in the minority in society."

Suddenly, I could see where he was going with this argument.

"There's one thing that can be done, but it will take generations. We have to increase the population of people with ASD. You know, grab market share."

"How is that possible?" asked Stef.

"Obviously, as a community of autistic people, we need to have a lot of unprotected sex. ASD is largely genetic. If the ASD community has a lot of babies, a fair percentage of them will probably have ASD. We'll aim to increase our population share by a percentage point at a time."

"And in five hundred years we might be twenty percent of the population," I said. "Unless, of course, genetic engineering in the future prevents us from reproducing."

"Yes," agreed Cliff, without looking at me. "In a millennium or two, we might dominate society. Lots of sex is the answer."

Chloe beamed at him. I could see the reflection from the bare light bulb glinting off her white teeth. She reached over and touched his arm again, just like she had done in the café earlier that day.

"That sounds like the Nazis," said Stef.

"It's natural selection. Survival of the fittest. Or horniest. That's all. And it's accomplished perfectly naturally, by sex alone. What do you think, Bobbie?"

"My name is Robert," I said, "and I am willing to help in this project as often as I can."

"That's great," said Cliff monotonously. "I knew I could count on you, Bob. Is there any dessert?"

"Oh, yes," said Chloe, bouncing to her feet. "There's always ice cream and fruit salad, or there might be a cheesecake in the freezer that we can defrost. Ooh, or I could make an apple crumble. Oh, but then we would have to wait. I'll get the ice cream." She rushed out to the kitchen. Cliff smiled broadly after her.

I grimaced, not really knowing why. My negative feelings about Cliff seemed to be returning.

Chloe rushed back with the ice cream container and an ice cream scoop in one hand, and a stack of four dessert bowls in the other. She plunked them down on the table unceremoniously and abruptly turned to face Stef.

"Oh, Stef, I forgot to ask before... Is it all right if Cliff stays the night? He's—"

Stef smiled widely. "You don't need to ask me, Chloe. This is your house too. Cliff can stay whenever you want." She looked directly at me and winked twice. Perhaps there was some grit or something in her eye. I frowned.

"Thanks, Stef." Chloe smiled broadly.

"Yeah, thanks, Stef," echoed Cliff without looking up. He dug into the ice cream with the scoop ferociously. It was vanilla, my favourite. Chloe's, too, though I think she tried strawberry once.

At that point, I probably scowled, but I am not sure, for no one commented on the fact.

Chapter Sixteen

Books read lately:
Manias, Panics and Crashes – Charles P Kindleberger and Robert Aliber (note: this is not about mental illness, anxiety and car accidents; it is a history of financial crises resulting from a mismanagement of money and credit, recently updated to cover the latest goings-on...)
Number of sexual encounters:
Now starting to lose hope entirely

Non-Spectrum Disorder (also known as Neuro-Typical (NT) Syndrome):
A pervasive developmental disorder thought to affect up to 99% of the population. According to the Directory of Sensory Maladies (DSM-V), Non-Spectrum Disorder may be diagnosed by observing all of the following characteristics:

1. Persistent deficits in social communication and social interaction with autistic people:
   1a. Conformative, rather than unusual, behaviour, including following fads and fashions, and watching television shows with an emphasis on emotive reactions in non-autistic people;
   1b. Tendency to self-expression, including using body language, gestures and involuntary facial movements;
   1c. Incomplete, non-literal, vague or misleading responses to logical questions and statements, at times

extending to dishonesty;

1d. Excessively seeks company of other, non-autistic, companions, extending to massing in large social gatherings, to engage in apparently meaningless activities (such as browsing in the mall, or 'small talk'), rather than spending time alone pursuing own special interests in depth;

2. Diverse, non-repetitive / random patterns of behaviour, interests or activities, manifested by at least four of the following:

2a. Avoidance of routine and repetitive actions; excessive variations of food, drink, routes taken, etc.

2b. Inability to fixate or perseverate upon interests; scattered and varied interests lacking obsession;

2c. Low sensory sensitivity to loud noises, visual stimulation, smells, tastes and touch (especially from other people);

2d. Inhibited or apparently repressed stimming behaviour;

2e. Tendency to touch others (particularly relatives), with apparent disregard for personal space and safety;

3. Symptoms must be present in early childhood (but may not become fully manifest until encountering people on the spectrum);

4. Symptoms together limit and impair everyday functioning with regard to people on the spectrum.

On Friday morning when I came downstairs, Stef was already in the kitchen. It looked like she was about two and a half minutes, or 62.5%, into her four-minute cereal breakfast. She looked up as I entered.

"What's wrong, Robert?" she asked between

spoonfuls.

"I am not aware of anything being wrong," I replied. That was the truth. I realised I was not smiling, though. In fact, I was scowling. I wondered for a moment if, perhaps, I had been scowling in my sleep the entire night.

"Grab a coffee. It'll do you good. Maybe even have two." Stef motioned with her spoon, dripping milk onto the tabletop.

I grunted in reply and went over to the bench to switch on the kettle. I stared outside the kitchen window at the creeping commuter traffic in the street, and at the spot in the garden where I had parked my scooter months before. I had never seen it again.

"Cliff is asleep in the living room," said Stef in a lowered voice. I had no reason to disbelieve her, but I still went over to the living room door and peeked through to see for myself. Cliff lay curled up, unmoving, on one of the orange sofas. How he could sleep on one of the most hideous and uncomfortable pieces of furniture ever made I did not comprehend, but somehow he had managed it.

"I don't understand," continued Stef, her spoon hovering over her almost-empty bowl. "I thought he and Chloe were, you know, together. Why's he sleeping down here?"

"She has not known him very long," I said, before realising that I actually did not know this for certain. The kettle switched off with a click, summoning me, and I went over to make my coffee.

"Oh, perhaps she isn't ready to sleep with him yet."

I fumbled the teaspoon, and it fell into the stainless steel sink with a jarring clatter that set my teeth on edge. I fished another one out of the drawer, finished making my drink and joined Stef at the table. She had not made much progress on finishing her breakfast.

"He's kind of opinionated, isn't he?" she whispered.

"He certainly is," I agreed. "And judgemental. And he likes the sound of his own voice too."

"Some of his ideas sounded a bit, well, wacky. He's not a pot-head, is he?"

"I do not know," I said, recalling what James had told me about Cliff, which did not include anything about drug-taking. "He seems a little crazy. Perhaps more than a little. I know almost nothing about him. I do not know what medication he is on, for instance." *And if he is not on something, he should be*, I thought.

Stef pursed her lips and nodded for a moment. "I just feel a bit uneasy about this guy, Robert. He's strange. I'm worried about Chloe getting involved with him. Do you know what I mean?" She looked up at me. "I suppose you don't. It's just a feeling I have. You probably don't get it."

"I do not get it, what you are feeling about him, I mean, but I do not trust him either," I said. "Can we just tell him to go away?"

"No, Robert, we can't. You see, Chloe is an adult, and she has to be able to make her own choices about these things. We can't make them for her. Also, if we send him away and she does fancy him, it might make things worse. She won't trust us, and she might go and stay with him. If he is a dodgy character, it would be much better if they are here, so we can keep an eye on Chloe and make sure she is all right. Especially as he will be her first real boyfriend."

"I understand," I said. I felt really down, even a little miserable, but I did not know why. I took a long swig of my coffee. Maybe it would help.

"Let's see what happens tonight," whispered Stef,

rising from the table and putting her bowl of unfinished cereal in the sink.

"I am not sure I actually want to know."

Stef paused by me on her way out of the room. She placed her right hand on my shoulder. She had done this before, many times, so I was used to it and did not flinch. "You know, Robert, you can have a friend or girlfriend to stay over any time you want, like if you start going out with someone, or even if a friend needs a place to stay for a few nights. You know that Wayne stays over here a couple of nights a week with me, and if Chloe is going to have someone to stay, it's only fair that you can, too. If you want to, that is."

"Thanks, Stef."

"Are you still looking for a girlfriend?"

"Yes, I am. It is my special project for the year. I thought I wanted a woman who is not on the spectrum and is quite normal in every way—"

"Whatever that means," sniggered Stef, withdrawing her hand from my shoulder and stepping back.

I do not know if that movement signified anything or not. Probably not, but how would I ever know? I continued. "But now I am not sure if an NS woman would be right for me. Finding a girlfriend seems almost impossible. I do not know how to begin. I am not like you, Stef. You are friendly and sociable and quite nice. Lots of people are attracted to you."

"Quite nice. Thanks, Robert, I know what you mean. You're a nice guy, too."

"Well, I have calculated that there ought to be one suitable woman in Christchurch for me, but I do not know how to locate her."

"Don't worry about finding a girlfriend. You'll meet the right girl sometime. Just wait and see."

She left the room and went upstairs, probably to finish getting ready for work. I stood at the kitchen sink drinking my coffee and looking out at the traffic again. It had moved along a few metres. After a few moments (*how long is a moment, anyway?*), an idea came to me. I stuck my left hand into my jeans pocket and took out a creased white card with a hand-scrawled mobile number on it.

I finished my coffee and called the number. It rang five times before it was answered.

"Hello? Who's this?" said a sleepy voice.

"It is Robert. Is that James?"

"It might be. Who are you, and why are you calling me at this time of the night?"

"It is seven-thirty-four am," I said. "On Friday. I am Robert. If that is James, you talked to me outside the café yesterday, remember?"

Silence.

"You talked to me about Cliff, remember?"

"Ah, got you. Cliff was with your girlfriend, wasn't he?"

"Chloe is not my girlfriend. She is my flatmate."

"Whatever. Do you have some information for me? Something about Cliff?"

"I know where Cliff is staying. He is at my house. Maybe for a few days. I do not know for certain how long for, but he is here at the moment."

Silence again, but shorter than before. "Why is he at your house?" asked James.

"Why, I really do not know. He is still asleep on one of our uncomfortable orange sofas."

"I hear you." I heard the sound of scribbling through the phone as James made some notes. "Has he been talking about his secret organisation and its plans?"

"Yes. He has been talking about that almost exclusively. Chloe just listens to his crazy ideas. I am her friend, and I am worried about her. She is quite easily influenced by people."

"Naturally, you're right to be concerned. Listen, I need to get closer to him. Cliff. To sound him out about what he's up to."

A suspicious thought entered my mind. "What secret organisation did you say you are working for, James?"

"Never mind. I really can't say. Best that you don't know. Now, where is your house exactly?"

I told him the address in Matipo Street, then added: "You are welcome to stay if you want to."

More silence, then: "You're asking me to stay with you?"

"So you can observe Cliff. You can sleep in the living room. Why not? He is."

"Ah, got you. That sounds great, thanks. I'll rock on over there tonight."

James arrived at 6.17 p.m. I brought him into the living room to meet my flatmates and Cliff, who was still hanging around like he owned the place. Before I could say much to introduce James, though, he spoke up to introduce himself. The moment he started speaking, everyone gave him their full attention. His voice was unusual and somehow captivating. He spoke clearly, smoothly and almost hypnotically. It seemed quite at odds with his scruffy and chubby physical appearance.

He did not introduce himself as James.

"I'm a friend of Robert's from Uni," he said, looking at everyone in turn. "Call me Jimmy. I'm a third year Psychology student. Should finish this year, I hope. I've seen you around the faculty." He nodded in a friendly manner to Chloe, who did not respond, and James, or Jimmy since that is what he preferred to be called, continued without a pause. "I didn't start Uni straight after school. I joined the army—French Foreign Legion, actually—as a paratrooper, but that led to my interest in studying psychology. Of course. I'm twenty-nine. Anyhow, it's great to meet you all. I hope Robert explained that he offered to let me stay because I need somewhere to crash for a few nights. It's kind of you."

"He didn't say anything about it," said Chloe. "And I've never seen you before, either at the faculty or with Robert."

"I keep to myself," explained Jimmy with a smile.

"You're welcome to stay, Jimmy," said Stef hurriedly. "I was talking to Robert just this morning about having friends to stay over. You'll have to sleep in the living room, though. It won't be very comfortable, but we have plenty of blankets, so you won't be cold. Did you say the French Foreign Legion?"

"Yes, but that's a long story. Thanks for letting me camp out here," said Jimmy. "The living room sounds just fine. Listen, I don't know if you've eaten or not, but I've brought dinner for all of us. I've got KFC, wine and cakes for dessert. How does that sound?"

Everyone agreed that sounded fantastic. Within a few minutes, we were all sitting around the kitchen table enjoying the food and drink that Jimmy fetched from his car. Especially the drink. Whenever we finished a bottle, Jimmy quickly opened another one. The KFC was soon devoured, and we moved to the living room for wine and cakes.

It did not take long before Cliff dominated the conversation with more of his bizarre theories and supercilious views on NS society. Chloe, usually not short for words, was silenced and seemed utterly transfixed by him and what he had to say. Jimmy also paid close attention to every word Cliff said and every gesture he made. I was surprised he was not taking notes.

After a while, Stef's boyfriend Wayne arrived and joined us. He and Stef talked and laughed together while Cliff droned on to Chloe and Jimmy. I felt isolated and alone, not truly part of, or interested in, either of the conversations going on around me.

Time wore on, and the effects of the wine increased. I started to feel sleepy and bored, and was about to go upstairs to my room when, in a rare lull, Stef suggested we all play a game while we enjoy the rest of the cakes and wine.

"Monopoly?" I suggested hopefully.

Stef grimaced, and Chloe swore. Ever since our marathon game of months before, neither of them had wanted to play again, but I kept trying.

"Cards?" suggested Wayne. "We could play Five Hundred."

"No, there are six of us," I said. "We need a special deck with elevens, twelves and thirteens, and we do not have one."

"How about Poker, then?" countered Wayne.

Chloe tittered. She had drunk five glasses of wine by now. Cliff frowned but said nothing. I wondered if he was unhappy that his diatribe against society had been interrupted by the suggestion of a game. I liked that thought, so I spoke up. Anything to keep him quiet seemed reasonable to me.

"Poker sounds fine."

"I don't have a bloody clue how to play it," moaned Chloe.

Wayne grinned widely. "It's easy. Look, we don't have to play for money, just for fun."

"Count me in," said Jimmy. "I won the Petone Poker Championships three years running."

"Is that while you were in the French Foreign Legion?" said Cliff.

"The online competition, of course," added Jimmy.

"Don't we have to take our clothes off or something?" asked Stef abruptly. She giggled and nudged Wayne in the stomach playfully, sloshing some of the wine in her glass over his dark sweatshirt.

Wayne laughed. Jimmy chuckled. Even the corners of Cliff's mouth twitched upwards in the semblance of a smile.

"How does that work? What are the rules?" I asked, intrigued.

Stef giggled again, her eyes glowing bright with wine. She looked up at her boyfriend.

"I don't know," he said. "I haven't played it like that. I suppose the winner of the hand chooses someone to remove an item of clothing, or maybe everyone except the winner should take off something."

"Wait! That's not fair!" said Chloe. We all turned to look at her inquisitively. "What if we aren't wearing the same number of items of clothes?"

"We should normalise the number of items we have," I said. No one seemed to be listening to me, though.

"That'll be more fun than ordinary poker!" sniggered Stef, ignoring me.

"What about socks?" asked Chloe. "Do they count as one pair or two single items?"

"One," said Wayne. "They're a pair, aren't they?"

Stef fetched a pack of cards from the small bookcase in the hall and suggested we play on the floor in the living room because there was more room to spread out there. I had played poker on the computer and understood the rules and odds, but the others were all novices, so Wayne spent three and a half minutes explaining the technical rules. Stef and Chloe just giggled and did not appear to listen at all. Jimmy was attentive and took some notes. Cliff just scowled and looked bored, but he assented to play anyway.

It required another ten minutes of preparation before we were actually ready to start, getting more cake and wine, positioning ourselves on the floor (Stef lay down, the rest of us sat) and agreeing on the final points of play. We decided the dealer would determine the game, and the winner of the hand would decide the clothes removal rule. We then drew cards to determine who would deal first, with the honour going to the highest card. That turned out to be me.

"Draw poker," I chose. It was the easiest game to play.

We played the hand and Chloe won it with two pairs, Queens and sixes. She shrieked with delight, causing me to cringe at the loud, high sound.

"Oh, what fun! I still don't even understand this game, and I've won! Robert, remove your shoes, please. What are these black clover things called again?"

"Clubs," said Stef, giggling from her prone position on the floor.

I took my shoes off as asked while Cliff dealt the next hand. "Texas Hold 'Em," he said. "You know, the game they show on TV."

I dropped my two cards when my piece of banana cake suddenly crumbled in my other hand and I tried to catch the debris, but no one minded or even looked at them. Jimmy won that hand with a full house and directed everyone to remove an item of clothing. For me, that meant both of my socks. My toes were white because I always wore footwear, inside and outside, regardless of the weather. I felt quite uncomfortable with naked feet and tried to sit with my toes turned under so as to hide them.

It was Wayne's turn to deal. "Texas Hold 'Em," he said, grinning as he shuffled expertly, "but with wild cards: twos, tens and one-eyed Jacks. That'll make it interesting."

"One-eyed Jacks?" echoed Jimmy, his lip curling up.

"The Jack of Hearts and the Jack of Spades are side-on, so you can only see one of their eyes," he explained, dealing.

I sighed. This was getting complicated.

Due to the preponderance of wild cards this time, everyone had a strong hand, but it took several minutes to work out what we all had. The worst of the hands was a straight but Chloe won with four sevens, two of which included the wild cards, the two of Hearts and the Jack of Spades. As soon as I explained she had won, she let out another high shriek of delight.

"I wish you would not do that," I said, cringing. My head was ringing like a belfry on Sunday morning.

"Sorry, Robert," she replied with a smirk. "Now take your shirt off."

I did so, feeling even more self-conscious than before.

Is Chloe deliberately picking on me? I wondered.

We played on, reverting to simple games at times and inventing horrendously complicated variants at others. I won a hand and took revenge on Chloe for targeting me with her stripping commands, though being the victim seemed to delight her just as much as being the victor.

By mid-evening, matters had degenerated further, and I wondered just how this was going to end. I hoped it would end soon. Only Wayne remained trousered, possibly because he had eased up on the wine, or maybe he was actually a decent card player. I was too sozzled to decide which. Stef had fallen asleep on the floor, and we thought it would not be right to continue playing a hand for her and remove her top and knickers when she lost. Jimmy did not appear to be as talented as he boasted—unless he was losing on purpose—as he was down to his underpants, the same as Cliff. They eyed each other with expressions I could not decipher, but mostly I gazed intently at Chloe. She sat leaning back, facing me, wearing nothing but semi-translucent dark green knickers and a matching bra, smiling and laughing, crossing and uncrossing her legs. While studying her, I wondered if the leg movements were some new way of stimming for her, but my thoughts drifted to my own uncomfortable situation, for I was also clothed only in my underpants, and they seemed rather tight. I sat perpendicularly to Chloe and prayed that I would not lose the next hand and be forced to reveal all.

Fortunately, at this point Wayne suggested ending the game to spare everyone's blushes—whatever that means.

C**HAPTER** S**EVENTEEN**

Books read lately:
Unwritten Rules of Social Relationships – Temple Grandin and Sean Barron
Number of sexual encounters:
Zero, zero, zero...

Chloe and I are different. That is, we are different to each other in a little way, but we are different to Non-Spectrum people in a big way. In her unofficial role as my 'therapist', Chloe has taught me that our brains are not wired the same as NS people.

You see, for NS people, the brain learns to do a lot on automatic pilot. The neural pathways form themselves into high-speed highways, making it easy to process lots of familiar information, such as recognising faces, determining what to do and say in particular situations, or making a balanced assessment of a combination of sensations coming through the five senses.

For AS people, the messages the brain receives tend to take the scenic route, on small, indirect pathways. For Chloe and I, this means it can take longer to process the same information, or that it may seem confusing or unfamiliar to us because we get it in disorganised chunks through several minor routes instead of all at once from a main neural highway. This can make it hard for us to process different things at the same time, such as what someone is saying and the movements they are making with their hands and face. When there is a lot of information bombarding us all at once, such as the sounds, movements and smells of several people, it is hard to know what is most important, and all the information tries to flow down the small, indirect pathways, and gets clogged up, just like a traffic jam. It is sensory overload. In addition, our sensory volume control tends to be turned up very high (a sound that is not loud to you might be unbearable to us, or a light too bright, or someone's perfume causes nausea), or very low (we might not notice if you talk to us, or if the temperature is very cold). We may need to block everything out for a while, just to let the brain catch up with its processing. We might rock, or tap our feet, or twirl our hair or just sit there in our own mental world for a while, making sense of it all.

I woke abruptly. A deep, rumbling sound filled my room. At first I thought it was a train, but the rumbling was far too powerful for it to emanate from a train passing through the crossing a few blocks away; besides, no trains pass through there at that time of the night. The sound grew louder and was joined by a plethora of other noises coming from all around me—rattling, banging, clunking, scraping, shouting. A terrifying thought occurred to me that maybe a heavy truck had crashed into the house, smashing the lower half of the building into matchstick-sized debris.

I flicked on the lamp switch and clamped my hands over my ears, trembling with shock. I looked around in astonishment, then realised it was not just me shaking—it was everything around me, everything in the room. My bed heaved beneath me like a grumpy steer at a rodeo. A picture hanging on the wall above my bed swung like a pendulum, scraping against the wall and leaving a black arc as a record of its motion. A small clock on a stand toppled forwards off the quivering chest of drawers, the dull thud of it striking the carpeted floor swallowed up by the general din. Books shook themselves out of the bookcase and tumbled to the floor. Fortunately, the bookcase itself was screwed to the wall, but it tried to burst loose. I had Sex on the bed and noticed that she was no longer curled up asleep, but standing up, the hairs on her arched back sticking up. She looked like an inverted hairy letter 'U'. She emitted a mewing sound like an agitated child crying as her head swung from side to side, taking in the mayhem around us, before leaping off the bed and bolting for the door.

I jumped out of bed. The floor was moving, jolting as the raucous noise increased in volume. I flung my arms out wide, trying to keep my balance, and cracked my right wrist painfully into the wall. I lurched towards the doorway, bounced off the wall with my shoulder, then banged my hip on the teetering chest of drawers. Pottery shattered somewhere down the hall, the tinkling sound standing out from the rough banging of shuddering furniture and the deep, growling, gravelly sound from the earth below.

Somehow I reached the door, jerked it open and stumbled into the doorway. I braced myself against the door frames but felt myself being thrown to and fro between them as the roaring vibrations intensified. I heard a woman screaming—I think it was Chloe. I shouted out "Earthquake!" but I could barely hear my own voice. Suddenly, my lamp light and the hall light went out. The house was plunged into blackness, the depth of which I had never before experienced.

A crashing, splintering sound came from Chloe's room. Suddenly afraid for her, I left the relative safety of the doorway and staggered into the hall towards her room. I managed only two steps in the darkness before stumbling forward and falling to the floor on my side, knocking the breath out of my body. I retched and rolled onto my hands and knees, scrambling along the hallway, one moment in contact with the wall and the next moment not so, as the entire house continued to shudder and shake with horrendous grating and cracking sounds. I may have called out to Chloe, but I did not hear myself.

The cacophonous vibrations abated a little, and I crept closer to Chloe's room as fast as I could manage on all fours. The rumbling died down, and the shaking transformed to a gently rolling motion that reminded me of the sensation of a boat at rest on the waves. I got to my feet and felt my way along the wall to the door to Chloe's room in total darkness. I could hear alarms going off outside and shouting elsewhere in the house, but I could not hear Chloe.

A flash of torchlight caught me in the face, momentarily dazzling me. I looked away.

"Are you all right?" called Stef. I could not see her, but the light seemed to come from the area of her doorway. Her voice sounded strangely high-pitched.

"Yes," I shouted. The torchlight allowed me to see where Chloe's room was. I took the last two steps at a bound and pushed the door open. It banged against something hard on the floor, possibly one or more books. I could not see anything in there, but I heard Chloe gasp and whimper.

"Chloe! Where are you?"

"On the bed. The bookcase fell over. It fucking nearly killed me!" Her voice turned into a shriek.

Stef appeared behind me with her torch and shone it into the room. With its pale light, I saw Chloe sitting on her bed, arms clamped around her knees, rocking steadily back and forth. Her room was a complete mess (by that, I mean more than usual). Her tall bookcase had crashed to the floor by her bed. The single small screw attaching it to the wall had obviously given way with the force of the earthquake. Books were strewn everywhere, covering the floor with a sea of novels. Seven of them were open and lying face down, their tales open to the carpet at random points.

I moved further into the room and reached across the toppled bookcase for Chloe. Stef followed me, lighting the way with her torch.

"Grab my hand!" I commanded, urging Chloe. With a soft whining sound and no other comment, she took it and steadied herself as I pulled her across the fallen furniture. She stepped on a copy of *The Hobbit* and slipped because of the poor friction of the fiction on the floor, but I had hold of her hand and prevented her from falling. She threw her other arm around my shoulder with a low murmur. Instinctively, I let go of her hand and lifted her up, one arm under her shoulders and one under her legs. She felt light, or maybe the stress of the situation lent me strength. Slowly, in the weak light of Stef's torch, I picked my way across the carpet of fallen books towards the door.

"Quickly," she urged. "I need to get back to Wayne. I left him crouching for cover under the desk in my room. He was pretty nervous. I'll try to encourage him out now that it seems to be over."

"Do you have another torch?" I asked. *I hope the batteries do not run out in this one. The electricity has not come back on.*

"There are candles in the kitchen. No other torches, though."

"Let's buy another one," said Chloe, an unusual timbre in her voice. She clung onto my arm with a fearsome grip as I carefully carried her down the hall. I followed Stef into her room and lowered Chloe's feet gently to the floor. She stood there, looking at Stef and her torch. Wayne sat on Stef's bed, shivering and shaking, completely naked. He was breathing in and out rapidly and shallowly.

"Are you frightened or cold?" I asked Wayne, but he did not reply. I glanced at Stef and saw that she, too, was naked. I had not noticed that in the darkness of the hallway, but there was enough torchlight reflected off the walls of her room for me to see. She saw my glance, handed the torch to Chloe and hurriedly donned a bathrobe that was lying on the floor. Then she grabbed another, helped Wayne into it, sat down on the bed next to him and gently put her arm around his shoulders.

Chloe stood quietly murmuring to herself, pointing the torch at the floor and twisting her hair around the fingers of her other hand. She wore long pyjamas and did not look cold. I was in shorts and a T-shirt. I stood next to Chloe, uncertain of what to do and whether I was expected to do anything. I decided to follow Stef's example and put my arm around Chloe's shoulders. She leaned against me, and I slowly eased us down to sit on the floor.

We sat like that for a couple of minutes in silence. Chloe seemed calmer now that she was holding the torch herself. She had it pointed at the ceiling, which reflected the light dimly around the room. Stef and Wayne sat cuddling quietly on Stef's bed.

Suddenly, Stef spoke up. "Oh, we forgot about Cliff and your friend, Jimmy. They're downstairs. We haven't heard from them. One of us should go and check on them."

I stood up. "I will go. I will get the candles too."

Stef nodded. "They're in the left-hand cupboard in the kitchen. The candles, I mean, Robert," she added, clarifying.

I reached for the torch, but as my fingers brushed Chloe's hand, she jerked it out of my reach. "You can't take the torch, Robert! It'll be pitch black without it! You bloody can't leave us here without the torch!"

"But you are just sitting here," I said. "I have to go downstairs. It will be safer for me on the stairs if I have the torch."

"Please don't take the torch! It's our only light." She would not give it to me, which was not logical, really.

"Okay, then," I sighed, giving up. I went to the doorway and through it into the hall. I waited a few seconds for my eyes to adjust to the low level of light that escaped the room with me, but it was not sufficient for me to see more than two metres farther. I thought about walking in the direction of the stairs and decided it was too dangerous to do that, as I could not see them and I might fall. Instead, I groped for the wall and slowly felt my way along it until I touched the bannister.

I clung to the bannister and took a step forward onto the top stair in almost absolute darkness. I moved so slowly and cautiously that my footsteps made no sound. From outside, I could still hear a couple of alarms that had been set off by the earthquake. Steadily and apprehensively, I made my way downstairs.

It must have taken me at least two minutes, but I reached the foot of the stairs safely and started to edge my way along the hall to the kitchen. I could not even see my hand against the wall, as it was so dark there. I think I had forgotten to breathe at some point and resumed with a deep inhalation.

I reached the kitchen. Some light from the night sky illuminated it gloomily, and I was thankful for the large window. I felt for the light switch and flicked it on, but there was no response. *Still no power. It might be off for hours, even days.* I stepped forward, feeling what seemed like broken biscuits beneath my feet, stubbed my bare toes against the base of the nearest cupboard and swore quietly and monosyllabically.

I reached up and opened the left-most cupboard door. I could not see anything inside, so I felt around gingerly. Some items had fallen over, but nothing had spilled out. The mess on the floor had come from another cupboard, probably the pantry. My fingers touched a large, fat candle. I withdrew it gratefully, sat it on the counter in front of me and reached up to feel for the matches. Eventually, I found them nestled against the side of the cupboard.

Moments later, I had the candle lit and, using the light it cast, I headed for the living room door. It was closed. Cautiously, I opened it with my free hand, concerned at what I might find in there. Would the television have survived the quake, or fallen over and smashed? What of the bookcase holding Stef's grandmother's china—surely those irreplaceable items would all have been shaken off and shattered. And what of Cliff and Jimmy? Were they hurt, or afraid? Were they still there, or had they run outside?

The door swung open silently. The candlelight was supplemented slightly by starlight coming through the living room window, but everything was indistinct. A groaning sound came from the sofa on which Cliff had been sleeping.

He is injured, I thought, stepping into the room. *And where is Jimmy?* In the gloom, I could see the nearest sofa was empty. *Perhaps Jimmy has gone outside.*

After another step, I started to distinguish amorphous shapes in the room. I could see the outline of the other sofa. There was movement on it. The moaning sound came again. *Cliff, hurt.*

I took another step, but I did not say anything or call

out, and I did not really know why. I just had an unfathomable feeling that I should keep my silence. I raised the candle to see better.

That is when I saw them both. Cliff and Jimmy. On the sofa together. Clinging to each other.

I decided there was no need to ask them if they were all right. I turned around and made my way out of the room, closing the door behind me quietly.

I returned to the kitchen, searched the cupboard for more candles and found two. Holding them in one hand and the lighted candle in the other, I returned upstairs to Stef's room.

"I found the candles," I said as I entered. Of course, that was entirely unnecessary. They could see I had candles with me.

"Great," said Stef. She was still cuddling Wayne, who looked extremely pale in the torchlight and candlelight. Chloe sat apart from them on the queen-sized bed. Sex had come back from somewhere, and Chloe was stroking her comfortingly.

I placed the lighted candle on the bedside table. As it was so fat at the base, it stood by itself, but another earthquake might topple it. I did not want that to happen, as it might set fire to the bedsheets, so I put Stef's alarm clock and a book on either side of it for extra stability. Then I lit the other two candles from the first and propped them up elsewhere in the room.

"I'll switch off the torch to save the battery," said Chloe, and she did. The candles gave a low level of flickering illumination, but it was enough for us all to see each other.

Wayne spoke for the first time since the quake. His voice was hoarse. "Did you see Cliff and Jimmy down there?"

"Yes," I replied.

After a few moments, Stef asked, "And how are they? They're not dead, are they?"

"No, they are not dead. They were lying on the sofa together, kissing."

"What?" burst out Chloe. "Cliff and Jimmy? They were doing what?"

"They were kissing," I said, louder this time.

"Shit!"

"On the sofa? *Our* sofa?" said Stef. "Kissing? Were they doing anything else on it?"

"I could not see clearly, and I did not ask them."

"Probably just as well!"

"Shit!" said Chloe again. Wayne just laughed and shook his head. He seemed to be recovering.

I went to sit by Chloe on the bed. We were still sitting there comforting each other a few minutes later when the first of the big aftershocks hit. We had all talked about this and expected further quakes, but the crashing sound and violent shaking caught us by surprise, regardless. Chloe whimpered and buried her head deep in my shoulder, clasping me desperately with both arms as she let the torch slip out of her grasp. I held her tightly.

It was shorter and not as severe as the first one, but the noise itself was deafening. On it went, like underground thunder, for what seemed like ages but was probably only twenty or thirty seconds. There were no more crashing sounds from around the house. Probably everything that could have toppled over or fallen off shelves had already done so with the first major quake. We sat, clinging to each other, with the ground itself roaring at us as if in fury.

It passed. Silence descended on our little group for a

minute or so while we waited tremulously to see if another one would start up. Finally, Stef spoke up.

"It's just after five a.m.," she said. "Why don't we all go back to bed and try to get whatever sleep we can? We can sort out the house in the morning."

I nodded. That seemed fine to me. I picked up one of the fat candles with my right hand and clasped Chloe's trembling hand with the other. We left the torch and the other two candles with Stef and Wayne.

Slowly I edged along the hallway, almost dragging Chloe with me. We reached the doorway of her room and looked inside. Chloe gasped and sobbed. I had forgotten what a mess it was. Books and other items from the toppled bookcase littered the floor.

"I don't want to sleep in here by myself, Robert," moaned Chloe. She clawed at my arm, gripping it with vice-like fingers to prevent me from leaving her. "Look, I'll have to climb over the bookcase and all that other stuff just to reach my bed. And I can't have a lighted candle in here! It might fall over and set the books on fire! But it'll be pitch black without it. Can I sleep in your room? Please?"

"Sure," I said. I remembered how Chloe had slept on the floor in my room to look after me when I had been suffering from post-hypomanic depression. "But we will not easily be able to get your mattress out. You can sleep on my bed, though, if you want."

"Cool," she said, and nudged me with her elbow. I thought that was deliberate, but then realised another aftershock had started, and she had lost her balance and stumbled against me. A loud rumbling, cracking sound came out of the darkness. I bumped against the wall and almost dropped the fat candle. It probably would have gone out if I had.

The aftershock eased and then faded away to an eerie silence after a few seconds.

"Come on," I whispered, and guided Chloe down the hall to my room. Once inside, she pulled back the duvet on my bed and scampered into it, pulling it up around her neck as she curled up into a ball.

I set the fat candle down carefully on the bedside cabinet, propped it there with books and left it burning. The flickering flame resulted in unusual patterns of light and shadow playing across the walls. I watched them for a few moments before getting into bed. I knew the moving shadows would disturb me, so I closed my eyes tightly.

In the dark, in bed, I reached out under the covers with my right arm. I found Chloe's shoulder and let my hand rest there for a few moments. She did not move or say anything, but I detected a change in her rate of breathing.

I slid over and draped my arm around her. Her nightgown felt soft and smooth, and through it, I could feel the warmth of her body. It was comforting for both of us.

We stayed like that, dozing between the aftershocks, until 7.14 a.m.

Chapter Eighteen

Books read lately:
The Go-Go Years – John Brooks and Michael Lewis (note: this is not about the peak years of discotheque dancing; it tells of the volatility and drama of 1960's Wall Street and is much more interesting than disco...)
Number of sexual encounters:
As before, still none...

***stim** – to self-stimulate, especially with regular, rhythmic movements of parts of the body. Everyone does this occasionally, such as twirling their hair or tapping their feet. In people with ASD, this behaviour is more pronounced, more frequent and may appear (to NS people) quite odd or even weird. Methods of stimming include tapping feet, jiggling legs, clicking fingers, nail-biting, pulling or twirling hair, head-banging, grimacing, clapping, gesturing, pacing or rocking, but each person is different and may use several different methods. Stimming serves several functions, including blocking out the bombardment of external stimuli and providing a way for the person to exert control. People with ASD are generally highly sensitive and often find it difficult to process all the sensory input simultaneously, resulting in stress, anxiety, even meltdowns. It is calming and grounding to be able to take control of what your senses are experiencing by doing something as simple as rocking or tapping your feet.*

Bizarrely, we ate breakfast at the table that morning as if it was a normal Saturday morning, though we did not talk much. We all needed a break from talking. At least I did. The phone had at last stopped ringing. Stef had talked to her sister Marinda and her mother. Chloe's Dad had called her from wherever in the world he now was; Vienna, I think, or maybe it was Siena. Somewhere with a horse race, anyway. And my mother had called me to say she was all right, and her house had only a few minor breakages, and she was going to bake shortbread and afghans, and did I want any? I had said 'no'.

The kitchen floor was a mess as the pantry doors had been flung open and containers of rice, pasta and biscuits had spilled out, coating the floor with their contents. A carton of long-life milk had fallen and leaked by the cupboard, creating a pool of slurry sludge that Sex licked at enthusiastically. Two mugs had broken handles, but everything else was intact. We left footprints in the rice grains, pasta and broken biscuits layering the floor because we had not swept them up. It seemed too weird to do that yet, as if it was easier to ignore the disorder and pretend the earthquake had never happened. But this was actually impossible. Whenever we moved about, or even if I shuffled my feet, there was a crunching of food particles underneath our shoes, which I did not like. The power was back on at our house too, and the television blared from the lounge a constant stream of earthquake news updates. Incredibly, no one had been killed in the magnitude 7.1 quake.

"Where's Cliff?" asked Chloe, breaking the silence between us all.

"Wayne and I told him to leave early this morning. And your friend Jimmy, too, Robert. They're both troublemakers. I don't want them in this house, especially at this time."

Chloe was quiet for several seconds before she mumbled, "Yeah." It was quietest and shortest utterance I had ever heard from her, and she followed it with the longest sigh.

"You didn't know Jimmy very well, did you, Robert?" asked Stef.

"I met him two days ago. He sounded really interesting."

"He may not have gone on and on like Cliff did, but he did talk a load of crap," said Wayne.

"He apologised to me for that," said Stef. "He told me he's a post-grad psychology student doing his thesis on social proof. Basically, he's going around spinning ridiculous stories to gullible people—sorry, Robert—and observing what happens when they introduce him to their friends."

"I see." It was my turn to mumble, but before I could elaborate further, there was another short rumble and judder, over almost before we realised it had begun. The greatest reminder of the quake was the seemingly endless series of aftershocks. They kept coming and were completely unpredictable in their timing and magnitude. Some were sudden, loud, great rending tears in the earth beneath us. Much of Christchurch was built on a swamp and, at times, I wondered if the city would sink into it like Venice on super fast-forward. Other quakes were little jolts, over almost before we knew they had started. Yet others were quiet, rolling motions, the ground rippling like a lake reacting to a plopped pebble.

Though the aftershocks were all different, our individual reactions to them did not vary much. Stef said she was fed up with them and demanded to no one in particular (sometimes with coarse language) that they stop immediately, but with no effect. Chloe whimpered and curled herself up into a ball wherever she was if it was a big one, but quickly recovered when each was over, though she remained uncharacteristically quiet. Wayne rushed to the nearest doorway or dived under the table as each aftershock began. He did not say much either and was unusually pale.

I did not mind the quakes at all. If anything, I felt a slight rush of excitement as they struck, and felt bad after they were over in some undefinable way. Perhaps it was guilt that I was all right while my friends were upset, and elsewhere, possibly, people unknown to me may be hurt. Maybe I felt inadequate in some way because I did not have the same kind of emotional response as Chloe or Wayne or Stef. Instead, I felt that I was not really part of what was happening to us, that perhaps I was not even really there, though of course I was, actually.

Being Saturday morning, fortunately, none of us had to go to work or Uni. Luckily, the power was back on. We spent some hours tidying up around the house, interspersed with lengthy coffee breaks when we all sat discussing the earthquake, trying to process it in our minds. At least that is what I was doing.

Chloe and I spent most of our time clearing up her room. We stood the bookcase up and attached it to the wall again, this time much more securely than before, using eight screws, which were all we could find in the house's hardware box. We spent an inordinate amount of time returning her books to their homes on the shelves. Chloe insisted on putting them back in exactly the same places and wanted to check each of them individually for damage first (of course, I agreed with her about the necessity of doing this). Our efforts resulted in slow progress, and this was further hindered by frequent aftershocks that caused Chloe to abandon her searching and sorting and take refuge by curling up in the doorway.

It was a day unlike any other in our lives. By the end of it, we were physically and mentally exhausted from our tidying efforts and the relentless aftershocks. However, we were among the lucky ones. A state of emergency had been declared across the city. A large proportion of the CBD had been destroyed or was damaged beyond repair. Much of the city was without power and water still, and thousands of people were staying with friends or in temporary shelters.

I went upstairs to bed at 9.17 p.m., quite early for me, to read *The Big Short*. Stef, Wayne and Chloe had already gone to bed, tired and stressed. Wayne was staying overnight again. His own house had no water or power.

I had been reading only a few minutes, with Sex napping next to me, when there was a knock on the door. Chloe came in without waiting for me to answer, dressed in her pale blue nightgown and twirling her cobalt blue hair.

"Are you okay?" I asked. I did not think she was. Normally when she comes into my room, she has her laptop or a book, but this time she had neither.

She came right over to me and sat on the edge of the bed. "No," she said, shaking her head. "I don't want to sleep in my room, Robert. I just can't. I can't even read in there or work on my web app. And when I close my eyes, all that's in my mind is the terrible sound of the earthquake, of the bookcase crashing over and everything falling out. It's scary, Robert. What if it all happens again tonight?"

"It might do, but the bookcase should not fall over this time," I said. "It is attached to the wall much more securely now."

"I know that," said Chloe, making a face, the meaning

of which I could not decipher. "I know it's not going to fall over. That's not the point."

"Then what is?"

Chloe's mouth turned down as if she were about to cry. "I'm frightened, Robert. I've never been scared like this before. It just doesn't seem safe anymore, even to close my eyes and sleep. I don't want to be on my own."

I nodded, showing that I knew what she meant, even if I did not feel the same way myself.

"Can I sleep in here tonight?"

"Sure," I said, expecting her to go and fetch her mattress and drag it into my room, but she did not do that. She swung her legs up onto the bed, crawled over me and settled herself into bed on the other side, her legs under the covers.

"Thanks, Robert," she said, smiling broadly at me over the curled-up kitten. "I already feel much safer, being with you. I just couldn't stay in my room any longer by myself. I kept staring at the bookcase, expecting it to topple over again, and I'm afraid to be alone if there's another big earthquake."

"It is okay," I said, returning the smile. A thought occurred to me. "Do you want to..."

"Do I want to do what?"

"Do you want to read?" I concluded, though already I knew she would not want to read. She had not brought her book in with her.

"No, I'll just sit here and stim for a while until I've calmed down." She closed her eyes and started rocking her head back and forth a little, as she often does when she listens to a song on her iPod, but she was without music this time. The duvet also moved slightly. I think she was wiggling her toes.

I read more. After a short while, I noticed Chloe slip down under the covers. She lay there quietly for a few minutes while I continued to read, but soon after that I felt her foot caressing my left leg. I shuffled over slightly to give her some more room.

"Robert." Her voice was a whisper. "Robert, do you want to have sex?"

"She is right here, Chloe. She has been dozing while I read, as usual."

Chloe's hand shot out, and there was a sudden yowl as Sex was roughly roused and pushed off the side of the bed. She stalked off, hissing, and lay down on the pile of clothes I had laid out for the morning.

Chloe emerged from the covers and peered at me. "I meant, do you want to have actual sex?"

I closed my book and lay it on the bedside table by the lamp before replying. "Of course I do, Chloe. It is my special project this year, but I have not found a prospective partner yet. You know that."

"No, Robert, I mean: do you want to have sex with me?"

I looked at her incredulously, not knowing what to say initially, then I said the first thing that came into my head.

"Yes. I do. I really do." And even as I said it, my body responded to the thought of making love with Chloe, to the anticipation of the close skin contact with her, to exploring her body and her sexuality with the utmost intimacy. If only I knew how to do it.

"Let's do it, then." Chloe rolled over closer to me, wrapping her left leg and arm over me. "You know I've always fancied you, Robert."

"No, I did not know that," I replied. *I wish she had said something about this ages ago. How was I supposed to know?*

"Do you fancy me, Robert? Even a little bit? I know you want a 'normal' girlfriend"—she accentuated the word 'normal' to give it a pejorative emphasis—"but, hey, we're friends, we spend most of our free time together, we laugh together, we study together, we walk together, we share everything except a bed. And now this bloody earthquake has certainly made me think, Robert, to think about my life, about what life's for. Up to now I've only been thinking about what I don't want. I don't want to be alone. I don't want to be ostracised and treated like a weirdo. I don't want to spend countless hours developing *hatelist.net* anymore. Instead, I've been thinking about what I do want. I want to get my psychology degree, of course, and finish *hatelist.net* eventually, but mostly what I want is to share love with someone who truly understands me and accepts me as I am, warts and all. Do you know what I mean?"

"I did not know you had warts," I said. "Where are they?"

"No, no, I was speaking figuratively. Figuratively. Not literally. I don't have any warts. It's just one of those crazy things people say."

"Right," I said weakly. I vaguely remembered her telling me about figurative speech and metaphors and so on a while ago, but I really did not feel like a refresher lesson just now.

"What I actually mean is that I want to choose someone—a partner—who will take me without judging me by my past, without trying to change me in the present, and without limiting me in the future. I know you won't do that, Robert. And you've come a long way yourself. You're not the shy, withdrawn young man you were when I met you. You're more confident, happier and calmer. You cared for me so nicely last night after the earthquake. I've never felt safer with anyone and more trusting of anyone than you, Robert. I've always fancied you a bit, but now it's a lot. I want you, completely and totally. How about you? Do you want me?"

"Yes," I said. There was no point denying it. I knew at once that it was true. My voice sounded strangely hoarse and throaty. My head felt light, probably because lots of blood had rushed to another part of my body. All year I had tried to find a girlfriend, but I had not seen the obvious, the wonderful woman with whom I spend most of my time, my best friend, the woman now lying in bed next to me.

"You do want me," said Chloe, moving her leg so her thigh brushed higher up my body, and pushing her hand under my T-shirt to stroke my chest gently. "It certainly feels like you do, anyway."

"Yes, I do," I said, reaching out for her, embracing her and pulling her closer. I knew it then, without doubt. "I do want you, Chloe. I've always wanted you, but I've never realised it. You're the perfect woman for me. You're so intelligent and interested in all sorts of things. We can talk for hours on almost anything, like historonomics—"

"Or evolution or string theory or parallel universes," she reminisced.

"And you're so funny sometimes. You know, I've enjoyed every moment I've been with you. And you can see me. The real me. Oh, I've been so stupid. I've never realised that you'd fancied me at all, let alone for so long. And you're right, we do share everything except a bed."

"And now we do. And you know something else, Robert?"

"What?"

"You're not talking as pedantically as you usually do. You're speaking with contractions."

"I'm not, am I? Oh, yes, I am. I'm doing it now. But...why?"

Chloe drew herself back and smiled at me sweetly. "I think it was like a mental shackle you'd put on yourself, Robert, and now you've found the key and released yourself, just like someone who suddenly stops stuttering when they remember and understand the incident that caused it to start. And you are free, Robert. We're both free to be ourselves, with each other. Now," she said, squirming back into my embrace and stroking my shoulder with her left hand, "how about making love? It'll be the first time for both of us, right?"

I answered her with a kiss that I judged to be passionate, and tried to remember how I had seen it done on TV and in the movies. There seemed to be so many different ways, and I wasn't exactly sure how to proceed. I kissed Chloe even more deeply and started to run my hand over her back. She giggled and responded by wrapping her legs around mine tightly.

"Ow," I said. "You scratched me with your toenail."

"Sorry. I didn't mean to." She pulled herself up on top of me. I could feel the firmness of her breasts pressing down onto my chest. No doubt she could feel something too. I could hardly believe this was happening.

"When should we take our night clothes off?" I asked. "Now, or later? Do we have to strew them all over the floor like in the movies?"

"Hmm, I don't know when. We can be tidier, though. Here, let's take them off now and put them next to the bedside table."

It took us only ten seconds to remove our clothes, and another fifteen for Chloe to lay them out neatly on the floor. She rolled back onto the bed and, as I moved towards her at the same time, our heads bumped, painfully.

"Oooh," she said, lying back. "That hurt."

"Maybe that's what's meant by unsafe sex," I said, rubbing my forehead.

Then we forgot about our pained heads, and we were cuddling each other again and kissing wildly. I had never seen Chloe like this, and she drew responses from me that I never knew I had. She kissed my neck, my shoulders, my chest. I thought it sensible to respond in the same way, so I performed the same sequence of kisses on her.

"Oh, Robert, that's good! I never knew it would be this nice!"

I climbed on top of her and reached underneath her with my arms, continuing our lovemaking in the way I thought it was performed in the movies, though usually camera angles and sheets prevent the pertinent bits being shown, and also perhaps with less noise than in the movies. Our passion increased. At least I felt that mine did. Chloe seemed to be responding in kind.

"Oh, Robert! Oh! Oh! Oh!"

"Chloe!"

"Your watch band is biting into my shoulder blade!"

"Sorry." I rolled to the side, unclasped my watch and put it gently on the bedside table on my book, where it would be safe. I rolled back to embrace her again. Our passion returned, and I entered her. It was a remarkable sensory feeling.

"Oh, Robert, it hurt when you did that!"

"Do you want me to stop?" I asked. *Please say 'no'.*

"Are you crazy? I think it's supposed to hurt the first time. Keep going! All the way!"

This time there was no stopping us. Minutes passed as we held each other more tightly, moving our bodies in a rhythm together unlike any I have ever known. I stopped thinking about how it is done in the movies. I stopped thinking altogether, actually, as I became immersed in the action of our intimate physical union. Finally, my moment of intense pleasure engulfed me. I breathed a huge sigh of relief and slid off to the side, embracing Chloe affectionately.

"That was fantastic," I said. "I never knew it would be so good!"

"Was it?" asked Chloe, a little breathlessly. "Are you finished? But I haven't had an orgasm yet."

"Why not?" I asked, suddenly doubtful. Perhaps the movie stud performance that I thought I had given had not been up to par after all. "What happened to yours?"

"I don't know. It just didn't...happen. Aren't I supposed to have one too?"

"Well, in the movies usually both people have them at the same time. So...was mine early or is yours late?"

"I don't know, but I don't think it's going to come along now that we've stopped. Can't you get back on for a bit?"

I took stock of myself, both physically and psychologically. At least one of those stocktakes was negative. "Sorry, I don't think I can," I said apologetically.

"Maybe you did it wrong," said Chloe. "It was your first time, after all. Maybe you're just not any good at it yet."

"It was your first time, too," I retorted, rolling to the side and releasing her from my embrace. "Maybe you didn't do it right either. I mean, yourself."

"I'm disappointed. I expected more than that. It was nice, sure, but you got a lot more out of it than me. That's not fair. And I'm the one who might get pregnant."

I looked at her, horrified. "Are you?"

"Am I what?"

"Are you pregnant?"

"I don't feel any different. Maybe it didn't work this time."

"That's good," I said, exhaling audibly with relief.

"Maybe it takes a while to be certain. But, hey, what are we going to do next time? How can we get it right in the future? I want to have orgasms too."

"Of course you do," I said, somewhat guiltily. Maybe I had been deceived by the movies, which made sex look rather easy and natural. It seemed to be more complicated than that. "Maybe I can ask Doctor Meg to explain sex to us, so we know what to expect."

"Sure. That'd be fine, but what about now?" She leaned towards me and looked at me in a strange way with her eyes rolled up. "We might want to learn before her next available appointment."

"I suppose we can google it to find out what we did wrong and how to improve."

"Good idea, Robert," said Chloe, sitting up abruptly. "Go get your laptop. Let's research."

My laptop was on my desk, and I fetched it immediately, smiling. There was almost nothing that Chloe liked more than googling for information. This will cheer her up, I thought. Maybe she'll not mind about the missing orgasm once we get stuck into the research.

I slid back into bed next to Chloe and flipped up the screen of my laptop. She put her right arm around my waist and rested her head on my shoulder. Swiftly, I opened up Firefox, went into Google and typed 'sex' into the search box.

I paused. "Shall we try 'I'm Feeling Lucky?'" I asked.

Chloe shook her head. "No, just do the normal full search. Let's see what comes up."

I clicked 'Google Search' and gasped in surprise as the search engine returned a list headed by 'About 2,830,000,000 results'.

"What's that number? How many is that?" asked Chloe, lifting her head off my shoulder. Her dyscalculia made it difficult for her to process sequences of digits.

"Two billion, eight hundred and thirty million."

"Fuck!"

I looked at Chloe inquisitively. "Should I try searching on that keyword instead?"

"No, no, I mean, that's too many. Let's narrow it down and see what we can find tonight."

"Wait a minute," I said. "Maybe there's a standard textbook for this somewhere. You know, an introductory primer. We should look at that first."

"I could ask Stef. She's probably read it. Hey, maybe she's even got a copy."

"Good idea."

Chloe got out of bed, donned her nightgown and went down the hall to Stef's room. I heard her banging on the door and entering. While I waited for her to return with whatever information she could find, I thought I may as well do something, seeing as I had my laptop open, so I had another look at *hatelist.net* to see what changes she had made recently. She had changed the title to 'late shit', yet another anagram. That made me laugh, but before I could investigate further, Chloe returned carrying three books. She shut the door behind her, pulled off her nightgown and slipped back into bed, smiling.

"She was a bit cranky because I woke her up, but she said I could borrow any of her books. She's got eleven books on sex. I picked three of them. Look, these ones have got pictures and everything. Just what we need."

"Did she ask why you wanted them?"

"Yes," giggled Chloe, "but I didn't tell her. I just said 'good night' and left. She can wonder about it. We'll tell her in the morning."

EPILOGUE

Books read lately:
No time to read
Number of sexual encounters:
17

Four days later...
I've decided to conclude my diary at this point. I don't have the time anymore to write in such detail. It is hard to concentrate with the earth moving so much (including the earthquakes). I've looked back to the beginning of the year, to when Chloe first suggested I write this diary, and it all seems so different now. I seem so different. My special project for the year was to find a girlfriend, and I have. Chloe is the best girlfriend I could imagine having. How strange I was unable to see this at the time when we first met.

In addition to finding a girlfriend, I've found myself. I've accepted myself. I've learned that it's okay to be different. In fact, if I could take a magic pill to become 'normal', I wouldn't. Why would I? This is how I am. If I wasn't like this, I wouldn't be me.

It's not about being who everyone else wants you to be, it's about being yourself and finding someone who loves every bit of it.

ABOUT THE AUTHOR

I've been writing off and on approximately forever. I'm middle-aged in a chronological sense, but young at heart. My favourite genres to read are speculative fiction and YA, but I also read some contemporary and some non-fiction books. My favourite author is Connie Willis, but I mostly read indie authors nowadays. My other interests include editing, hanging out with other writers, walking, playing backgammon, dancing Ceroc and spending time with my two boys. I also enjoy copy-editing and proofreading other authors' manuscripts.

I've co-authored three humorous fantasy books with Diane Berry: **Dragons Away!** (on the strength of which we won the Sir Julius Vogel Award 2012 for Best New Talent), **Growing Disenchantments** and **Fountain of Forever**.

Where I live

Christchurch is a city of approx 400,000 people on the east coast of New Zealand, which is about as far away from anywhere else as it is possible to be.

In September 2010 and February 2011, Christchurch was ravaged by major earthquakes that left much of the central business district in ruins, thousands of people homeless and some parts of the city uninhabitable.

But some of us are still here, writing.

Co-authored with Diane Berry as K. D. Berry:

Dragons Away!

YA Humorous Fantasy

Only one thing can beat a dragon and that's a bigger dragon. Just his luck that Drewdop is stuck with the job of finding one.

Growing Disenchantments

YA Humorous Fantasy

Releasing the world's most powerful magic talisman aided by an unwilling thief and with a distinct lack of forward planning. What could possibly go wrong?

Fountain of Forever

YA Humorous Fantasy

Time is on the move, mysteriously. Vilnius Baccarat desperately needs some of it. Can the Fountain of Forever save him before his time runs out?

An excerpt from

Misplaced

by **Lee Murray**
reprinted with permission

The make-up girl has a silver nose ring and hair streaked psychedelic orange.

'Almost done,' the girl says, puffing his face with powder. She has bony knuckles like cauliflower stalks. Holding his breath, Adam wills himself not to fidget as she deals to the fresh eruption of zits on his forehead. Right now, a few spots are the least of his worries.

'There, that's put some colour in your cheeks.'

Adam opens his eyes, stares at the mirror, and doesn't say anything. Even with the powder, he's as pale as Colgate. There's fuzz on his chin and dark bags under his eyes. He looks like a druggie, a metal-head on a bender.

The Powder Puff girl selects a lipstick from a tray which, held vertically, could be a Connect Four player board.

Resolution Red.

With a practised twist, she pushes up the tube.

'Pucker up, now,' she coaxes. 'Give me your sexiest pout, the one the girls love.' But Adam clamps his mouth shut, pursing his lips in a thin line, and shakes his head. No lipstick. This isn't an audition for

American Idol.

'But...' The Powder Puff girl puts on a pout of her own.

'No!' he says, with more vehemence than is warranted.

The girl shrugs, rolls her eyes. 'Whatever.' She packs up her Connect Four box and leaves him there.

'One minute, people!' the floor manager screams. Through the scramble of movement, Adam is aware of Dad, shuffling about on the spot off to the side of the make-shift set, a man out of his comfort zone. Six days a week, Dad's natural habitat is Creighton Cars, the yard that he runs. On Sundays, he mows the lawns, then slumps in front of the telly, cold beer in hand, watching whatever sport happens to be on.

Adam notices that Dad's tugging his earlobe again. Dad always does that when he's out of sorts. It's a good thing the clients haven't cottoned on or he'd never sell any cars. Lately, he's pulled that lobe so often it's a wonder he isn't mistaken for a tribesman from Borneo.

Not that Adam isn't uncomfortable. He wishes it hadn't come to this. The thing is, the news people insisted a public appeal could make a difference. They said it'd made a difference in other cases. But Dad couldn't face it, so Adam had agreed to do it instead. At this point, Adam would agree to car surf down Auckland's Queen Street in the wrong direction at rush hour, if there was a chance it would make a difference.

Anyway, it's better Adam does it because, being younger than Dad, he'll make the biggest impact, apparently. Adam knows this because he heard the camera crew chatting. They'd started off saying how Adam and Dad's story was made for television, the kind of story that won awards. Then one of them said it was a bummer that Adam was seventeen. That's when the guy holding the boom said, in these kind of cases, nothing tops a 7-year-old girl, especially a little blondie with dimples.

'Trust our freaking luck!' They'd laughed then, quietly amongst themselves, but one of them caught Adam looking and quickly shushed the others.

'Hey, show a bit of compassion, will ya?'

Maybe this is how his life will be from now on. People shushing each other or looking away. Feeling sorry for him.

'Adam? We're ready for you.' The floor manager speaks quietly. Adam's grateful. Right now, he feels like the entire cast of *Lost*, like something awful is about to happen. Maybe it already has, maybe he's living in a parallel universe and none of this is real, but whatever it is, Adam doesn't get any of it. He gets to his feet and allows the floor manager to direct him to the lectern. Placing both hands on either side of the lectern, Adam steadies himself.

This has to work. Please, let this work. Please.

But Adam knows that even if it does, nothing will be quite the same.

'In 5...4...3...' The floor manager holds up two fingers, then one...

The microphone makes a soft buzz as it's switched on. Adam pauses, marvelling at how they actually do that, the holding up the finger thing.

Oh shit.

He's on national television. His face spreads with warmth: the nasty-but-nice feeling you get when you pee in the sea. Great. His face will be red and blotchy now. He inhales deeply.

Swallows.

Stares directly at the camera lens.

What if this is the last time he ever speaks to her?

'Mum...Mum, if you're out there, if you can hear this, please, please call and let us know you're all right. Whatever's wrong, Dad and me, we're worried. Please, Mum, just come home...'

Printed in Great Britain
by Amazon.co.uk, Ltd.,
Marston Gate.